When Abe ta... ... ...
footba'l ... ...
is letting ...self in for. The team we.e imprisoned in ...
photograph by a witch and Abe has released them ...
the spell. The problem is, the team are now all old men—
but they act as if they were still 13 years old.

Abe decides the only answer is to take them home to
their families and he enlists the help of the beautiful Alicia,
the headmaster's daughter. But the boys' families have
gone long ago—and now the witches are trying to
recapture them. What can Abe do with eleven 13-year-old
old men who only want to play football? Can he stop
the witches? And will Alicia go on helping him, or is she
a witch as well? Abe's only choice is to go to Egypt to
find his father and ask him to help. But his mother has
always said that his father is a thief and in prison, so is Abe
only getting himself into even more trouble?

'. . . based on a brilliantly conceived idea . . . You will laugh and perhaps
cry as the old footballers look for their way home.'
The Bookseller

WILL GATTI has always enjoyed making up stories, and reading
them. Having daydreamed his time away at school, he gained
a BA(Hons.) in English at Oxford University and then had
various jobs, including being a warehouseman, a van driver, a
children's book editor, and an EFL teacher, before becoming an
English teacher. He lived on the west coast of Ireland for a
couple of years, then taught in Dublin, and is now head of
English at a school in Surrey. *Abe's Team* is his second novel for
Oxford University Press.

Other books by Will Gatti

Sea Dance
Jamboy

Abe's Team

Will Gatti

OXFORD
UNIVERSITY PRESS

F **OXFORD**
UNIVERSITY PRESS

Great Clarendon Street, Oxford OX2 6DP

Oxford University Press is a department of the University of Oxford.
It furthers the University's objective of excellence in research, scholarship,
and education by publishing worldwide in

Oxford New York

Auckland Bangkok Buenos Aires
Cape Town Chennai Dar es Salaam Delhi Hong Kong Istanbul
Karachi Kolkata Kuala Lumpur Madrid Melbourne Mexico City Mumbai
Nairobi São Paulo Shanghai Singapore Taipei Tokyo Toronto

With an associated company in Berlin

Oxford is a registered trade mark of Oxford University Press
in the UK and in certain other countries

Copyright © Will Gatti 2002

The moral rights of the author have been asserted

Database right Oxford University Press (maker)

First published 2002
First published in this paperback edition 2003

British Library Cataloguing in Publication Data available

ISBN 0 19 275294 4

1 3 5 7 9 10 8 6 4 2

Typeset by AFS Image Setters Ltd, Glasgow

Printed in Great Britain by
Cox & Wyman Ltd, Reading, Berkshire

PART ONE
THE PATH TO FORTUNE

ONE

The corridor was long and, at this time of the evening, shadowy and quiet. At one end a stone staircase led up to the dormitories. There was a pool of light down there because the staircase was lit. Then a gloomy bit. Then another pool of light. Then a gloomy bit. Then a pool of light, and in that pool of light there was a boy standing. He had his two hands on a cold radiator and he was swinging backwards and forwards, and as he came nose to the wall he tilted up his head and stared for a moment or two at the photograph hanging just above his head. Then he swung back out again, and his dressing gown made a swishing sound.

The boy's fingers were long and fine, the nails pale against the darkness of his skin. His eyes were dark too and there was something shadowy and uncertain about them, but his face was strong, good-looking in a hawkish way. He looked out of place in this silent school corridor; but he didn't feel out of place and that was simply because he was made to stand down there so regularly. He had a reputation, undeserved in his view, for not being good.

He was good, good at schemes for making money: fifty pence here, a couple of pounds there. He couldn't help it. The ideas just came, like the time he made tape recordings of his exclusive interviews with the stars of *EastEnders*. The first formers went for that big time, until one of his so-called friends spread the word that the interviews were fake. Of course they were. That was the point of schemes: they were ideas, they didn't have to be real. The money was real though. He kept that, saving it up for the really big idea, the secret plan.

Oh yes, it was the plan that kept him going, gave him something to daydream about during lessons or like now when he was stuck in the corridor with no one to whisper to, and too far from the dining room, which was at least another two pools of light down the corridor, to spy on the headmaster and his family, having their dinner.

The headmaster wasn't evil like most people supposed but he was bald and had what looked like shaving brushes sticking out of his ears. Perhaps that was why he boomed, because he couldn't hear himself otherwise.

Abe, the boy hanging on the radiator, didn't think much of the headmaster. He had been a captain in the navy and was a hopeless teacher, but his teaching wasn't the worst thing about him.

He employed other terrible teachers, some of whom fell asleep in lessons, some whose only skill was hurling chalk with deadly accuracy, and some who never ever smiled. And the headmaster, ex-naval captain Dunne, had chosen each one of them. Yet this too was not the worst thing about him.

The very absolute worst thing about the headmaster was his wife: Mrs Delia Dunne. Mrs Dunne ran the school. Parents loved Mrs Dunne because when she met them and took their little darlings by the hand, they saw a comfortable-looking woman, a little portly now but very good-looking, blonde hair swept back into a ponytail, and a warm, wide smile. 'So kind,' they would say, 'and so smart always.'

She wore sleek trouser suits that disguised some of her plumpness, a large black and gold ring on her right forefinger which some parents would find themselves staring at and then afterwards wonder why, and always she wore a blood-red silk scarf knotted around her neck. Abe knew there was something horrible about her neck. It was scabby, or flabby, or savaged with scars; or maybe it wasn't a real neck, but made of rubber, or of riveted metal.

'Don't be stupid,' his friends said. 'She just likes scarves, and doesn't like you. What's wrong with that?'

4

But Abe knew what was wrong: Mrs Dunne was evil. He could feel it in his bones, every time she came near, and he couldn't understand why everyone else didn't feel the same as him. It was true that the older boys, the ones in his year, didn't particularly like her. They said she was a bit weird but all teachers and their spouses were weird and he should shut up about it.

Weird! She was obsessive about how they made their beds, how they folded their clothes, and how they cleaned their ears. Nobody apart from him seemed to notice how when she was cross her neck and face turned crimson. Her whole face! Red chin, red cheeks, red nose, red eyes. It was as if she was burning.

Only evil people burned.

And whenever she came across Abe, she hissed just like a snake. Of course she never frightened the younger boys, with them her voice was like warm squishy fruit. They almost called her Mummy and they would do anything she said. Everyone seemed to do everything she said— everyone but Abe.

Abe did his best to keep out of her way but he watched her. At night she prowled the upper corridors in stockinged feet to catch them talking, and when she did she would murmur, 'Be sure to sleep tight, boys', and there would be instant silence and everyone would be asleep, except for Abe who kept imagining that she was still there behind the door, waiting. However, as Abe knew, Mrs Dunne had other pleasures, for after her late-night prowl she would join young Esther Chirt, the matron, and together they would have a glass of something green and exchange names of boys they disliked, boys who needed correction. And the boy named most often was Abe, which was why he spent so much of his time down in the corridor at night

His latest scheme had been particularly ambitious. At the school's front entrance was a circular bed of recently planted roses. Down the road was a garage whose owner was always offering odd deals on different things: one week umbrellas, the next charcoal, or apples . . . Abe offered him half a dozen young rose bushes at a good price. The man had winked and tapped his nose. 'No questions asked, eh?' And it was a deal.

Long after Mrs Dunne's midnight prowl, Abe had slipped out of bed, crept down the back stairs, and out of the boot-room door. He collected a spade and wheelbarrow from behind the big hedge where he had hidden them the evening before and, a little squeakily, wheeled his way across the drive. The moon was full, the sky clear, and a beautiful silvery light bathed the school grounds. Abe was in his element: a smart scheme, a good deal, a little adventure, money almost in his pocket which he would add to the one hundred pounds already stored away.

Except at the very moment that he dug his spade into the soil, there she was at the edge of the flower bed. Strangely, he couldn't now remember exactly what happened then, but he was sure she had said, 'Your mother told me to keep a special eye on you,' and she had certainly done that, and his ear had been very red and sore the next morning, as if it had been savagely twisted. And here he was now, down in the corridor, with a whole week of punishment ahead of him.

It was clear to Abe that she hated all boys, even the little ones, whom she pretended to mother, but he was sure that it was the older ones that she particularly hated. He didn't know why this was, and he didn't really care. What puzzled him was why she wasn't horrible to everyone all the time and why her punishments were so dull. Part of him almost wished she really was dangerous, and would threaten them all with withered arms, or with imprisonment in a dungeon from which Abe would have to make daring escapes. But she didn't. She was just . . . horrible and ugly, and standing in the corridor was boring; but then that was what boarding school was like most of the time. In fact until his spelling got some way under control he thought that 'boarding' was 'bored in'.

Abe's real name wasn't Abe, but Ebrahim; to be precise: Ebrahim Nasfahl Ma'halli. His friends called him Abe; the school and his mother called him Nasfali. 'Well, obviously I don't want you to have my family name,' his mother said, 'and you can't possibly have your father's. Nasfali will do.' So it did. He was half Egyptian and he spent much of his wasted time dreaming about the father he had never met and about Egypt and the long and winding River Nile, the Great Pyramid of Giza, the huge cities, and the wide deserts that he had never seen.

His father, so his mother told him, had been a liar, a cheat, and a thief and anyway he was dead and Abe was never to ask her about him again. Of course, Abe did and he asked about Egypt and Cairo too, and whether that was where he had been born, and whether he had uncles and aunts and cousins and could they go there and . . . Abe had been much younger when he had asked all these questions. He knew better now. His father had been a mistake, she said in that chill, dismissive voice of hers. Abe too had been a mistake; he should have been a girl. The first child in their family had always been a girl. Egypt had been a terrible mistake: it was too big, too messy, too full of people, too old and too foreign.

Abe's mother didn't like Egypt, that was obvious, and she also, like Mrs Dunne, didn't like boys. She didn't like her own son, either. It wasn't anything personal, she told Abe, just one of those things. His mother looked like a model: so slim she could practically thread herself through the eye of a needle; her hair was dark, her eyes were dark too, her neck was long and she had a way of looking down at people that made them feel that they were on the point of disappearing. She worked in something called a merchant bank, and nothing in her apartment was ever out of place—except for Abe.

As soon as he was old enough, she sent him off to boarding school, to Prackton Hall. If he was good and turned into a hard-working little drudge, she told him, he might become useful to her; if not, as soon as the law allowed, he could leave school, leave her, and, for all she cared, go back to where he was born, and beg in the million streets and alleys of Cairo. Now he was thirteen and his mother's threat was now his dream, his big plan for which he was saving all the money he could lay his hands on.

Abe swung back out from the radiator. He would go to Egypt, he would find out about this mysterious man, his father, and about his other family, he would ride across the desert under a full moon and (this was the best part of his dream) riding beside him would be the headmaster's daughter.

She was truly a mystery. Even his so-called friends agreed that there was something strange in the fact that booming ex-captain Dunne and his poisonous wife not only had a daughter who was beautiful but one who also seemed entirely normal.

'She is,' muttered Abe to himself, 'a vision.' He came nose to glass for the hundred and first time with the photograph of Prackton Hall's First Eleven 1942. Eleven boys in white shirts open at the collar and dark shorts, five of them sitting, and six standing. He knew them well. He knew all their names; he had even made up families for each one of them. He quietly chanted their names, his eyes shut, as he swung to and fro: Griffin, Roberts, Chivers, Thomas, Stokely, Bittern, Pike and Jonson, Jissop, Jack, and Gannet.

He opened his eyes and then stopped mid-swing and frowned. He shook his head. No, he had to be mistaken. Photographs don't change. All the boys in all the team photographs all looked serious. That was obviously how the photographer had wanted them to be. And so did this team, except for J. Griffin, the boy sitting on the far right.

How strange. He didn't look half as serious as the others, not if you looked close. In fact there was a clear hint of a smile in his eyes.

Abe pulled a face and swung out. Maybe he should move down the corridor and spy into the dining room and get a sneaky glimpse of the vision. Dangerous but undoubtedly worthwhile. The vision, like all visions, was seventeen, first year of A level at a local day school, and way out of the reach of Abe and his pals. Though that didn't stop her being the subject of much speculation and discussion.

'She's a babe.'

That was one entire, though much repeated, discussion.

'Her beauty knows no bounds.' That was after an incomprehensible English class. Not one of them could figure what 'bounds' meant but none disputed the 'beauty' bit. For a start her hair was shiny black and waxed into pixie points; her fingernails were always dark, mauve or blue, her eyes glittery and, best of all, she had a ring in her eyebrow, and one in her nose. Abe swore she had one in her belly button but his friends all beat him up when he claimed she lifted up her T-shirt to show him. Of course he was lying but he still believed she had one. How could she be their daughter?

'Adopted.'

'Stolen.'

'Perhaps Mrs D is a witch.'

This might have been a possibility except the only witches, the only real witches any of them had heard of, pottered around Stonehenge, or lived in little bendy houses down in Somerset. They didn't wear smart trouser suits and run boys' schools.

As for her daughter, had any of the boys actually spoken to her?

Abe tightened the cord round his dressing gown and pulled up his collar.

Not exactly. But there was always a first time. In three

seconds he had slipped ten paces down the gloomy corridor. Then the dining room door swung open and he froze.

'Nasfali! You horrible child, what are you doing sneaking about? Get back to your place.'

'Sorry, Mrs Dunne, I was just . . .'

'Nonsense!' she snapped, which was probably just as well because Abe had no idea what he had been about to say. 'Get over there. That's another thirty minutes, do you hear. Go up at ten o'clock and report to Miss Chirt. Not a moment before.'

Abe smiled and lifted his hand.

'What on earth are you doing, you stupid child? Anyone would think you were waving. Move!' Abe leapt backwards as if he had been struck by lightning, and swung round to face the photo, and grinned a huge grin.

The vision, otherwise known as Alicia Dunne, had stepped out behind her belligerent mother, had smiled and given him a wave, and the old thumbs up. 'Oh, bless the old thumbs up,' muttered Abe dreamily. Then he became aware of a thin voice, speaking as if from some distance away:

'Get us out.'

'What?' Abe swung round. No one there. Mrs Dunne and Alicia had vanished into the bowels of the kitchen. Out of what, he thought.

He turned back to the photo and pulled a face at his reflection. The boy sitting right in the middle, S. Jonson, pulled a face back. Then the entire front row pulled a face, while the back row turned round, pulled down their shorts and shook their bottoms.

Abe closed his eyes firmly, counted to ten, and then opened them again. He breathed a sigh of relief. The picture was back to normal, except . . . 'You're all in the wrong places,' he said softly.

'Regular Einstein, I don't think.' That thin, sarcastic voice again. He glanced back to the staircase, but he didn't expect to see anyone. It was one of the first signs of going mad, everyone knew that—hearing voices. 'First Joan of Arc and now me. And they burned her.' It wasn't a comforting thought.

'Come on, dumdum.'

'What do I have to do, Lord?' said Abe, his eyes tight shut. Of course, if it was voices then it was God. If it wasn't, then he was as barmy as a barn brush and it didn't matter who overheard him blathering like this.

'Get us out, of course.'

'Out of where, Lord? A burning bush perhaps?' He was trying to be helpful but he wasn't terribly up on Christian Bible study, since he had wangled his way out of it way back in First Year when Rajit said he should be allowed to study Sanskrit and he had muscled in on the act claiming he should be reading the Koran.

'Out of the blithering photo, you dummy.'

Blithering? What was 'blithering'?

He opened his eyes.

Two

He opened his eyes and all the boys in the photograph were in a huddle arguing and waving their hands. He could just make out bits of what they were saying: 'It's no good, he's stupid.' And: 'We can't stay here; I mean it's a blithering photograph. I'm thoroughly bored already.' And: 'Well, he's our only hope.' At this J. Griffin, who seemed to be the most active speaker, turned round and with his hands on his hips stared straight at Abe.

'How would you like to be stuck in a photograph and hung up on a wall?'

Abe was sympathetic. 'Depends how long for, I suppose.'

'How long for! For ever, that's how long for. Or until someone chucks us away. Think about it.'

Abe thought about it. 'At least you can move around and talk.'

J. Griffin momentarily looked puzzled. 'Yes, funny that,' then a little more briskly, 'but there isn't anywhere to go. What you see is all there is: just this bit of grass round us and then white nothing. But we reckon that you can get us out.'

'Why?'

'You're the only one who's seen us.'

'Have you tried to speak to anyone else?'

'There is only you,' said J. Griffin. 'So would you do us a bally great favour and let us out.'

'What do you mean, "bally"?' asked Abe. 'Nobody talks like that . . . '

'Nasfali! Are you talking to yourself, boy?' The headmaster's voice boomed down the corridor.

'No, sir, I mean a little bit, sir.'

'First sign of being a total whatsit. Wouldn't want to have to pack you off to a funny farm, old chap. Mrs D wouldn't like that at all.'

'No, sir.' Mrs D would probably like him torn apart by elephants.

The headmaster steamed off towards the private end of the building, clicking off the lights as he went. In moments, apart from the single pool of light around Abe, the corridor was dark. Perhaps he ought to be in a funny farm, whatever that was. At least it would be funny; this was so strange he didn't know what to think. He looked again at the team photos for 1941 and for 1943, nothing unusual about them: different boys, same sort of expressions, except theirs didn't move: no winking, no waving, no telling him what to do.

'Well?'

There was something irritating about this voice from the other side of the glass: thin, impatient, superior . . . and not real. How could it be? Much more likely to be indigestion, the solid sponge pudding they'd had for supper, or Mrs Dunne had drugged him. That's just the sort of thing she would do, so she could send him to a secret laboratory where they could perform medical experiments on him, and no one would ever know because she pretended to be such a mum . . . Stop! All he had to do was just move down the corridor a couple of steps and then that would be the end of it.

But he didn't. Instead he wondered what he would do with them if this was all real and he did let them out. How big were they? Two or three inches? He'd probably end up stepping on them. How about that? He could see the headlines: 'Boy squashes entire football team'.

Then he had another thought.

'Freaking pharaohs!' He could make a fortune: tour them round the country. It was a scheme of genius. Anyone his age would die to see them, money would pour into his cupped hand. They could be his team. Abe's team, he thought. He would end up fantastically rich and living in Cairo. Yes, indeed, a scheme of genius.

They would have to agree, of course. Perhaps they would want to go home. But they wouldn't have homes, would they? They'd be long gone, well, most of them anyhow. Sixty years. And even if their homes were there, they would still be only two inches tall. If they were lucky they would end up like pets, like Gulliver in the land of the giants.

He bit his lip. Maybe it was all more complicated than he first thought. Still, it was hard to feel that sorry for figures in a photograph, a black and white photograph too, even if they did talk to you. And anyway what would he think if he were in their shoes? Better a chance of freedom than a life behind glass, that's what.

'Well?'

If they agreed to do what they were told, maybe he could stow them away in his trunk. He could feed them scraps, a crumb would be a feast, wouldn't it? They would be so cheap. It was only a week to the end of term and then if they wanted to become millionaires, they could stay with him, and if they didn't they could set off on their own. That seemed fair to Abe, and he grinned, almost feeling the crinkle of fifty pound notes in the palm of his hand.

'All right,' he said. 'I'll do it, but you have to agree to what I say. No mucking about; I'm in enough trouble as it is.' And he told them how they would have to hide, and only come out when he said, and that he would take them back to his mother's apartment at the beginning of the holidays.

Abe and his mother had a businesslike arrangement. He came home for the holidays. She gave him a small daily allowance, left each day on the kitchen table in a brown envelope, and then he could do what he liked as long as his room was always tidy, he had had his evening meal before she came home, and he never asked her any questions. He knew other families operated in a different way to this but he was used to it.

'Yes, yes,' agreed J. Griffin. 'Now, how are you going to release us?'

'Take your photo out of its frame,' Abe said confidently. Well, it would either work or it wouldn't.

Abe unhooked the frame and lifted it down. Then he slid over the clips holding the back in place, pulled away a sheet of paper and then slipped out the photo. He turned it over. It was blank.

It was blank!

Not quite. The grass was there. So was the bench that the front row had been sitting on, but not one of the boys was there. In a panic, Abe pulled off his dressing gown and shook it in case they had got caught up in it somehow. Then he scrabbled down on his hands and knees, sweeping his hand across the floor. 'Oh no, no, please, I can't have lost them already.' He felt terrible. He was so careless. They would get squashed for sure, or eaten by the school cat.

It was just at the point that he was about to give up and plod upstairs when he became aware of voices, not the headmaster and his wife, nor those from behind the glass. Different. Who? And, what was more to the point, where?

As if in answer a light clicked on in one of the rooms off the corridor, just beyond the staircase.

'Shut the door!' The light disappeared.

They were in the changing room.

'Jumping jackfish!'

Someone snorted.

Then a soft little singsong voice murmured: 'I'm almost completely bald.'

And someone else said: 'Griffin, you blundering booby! Look at us!'

'It's impossible.'

Abe pushed open the door and . . .

Stared!

And they stared back. They? They! Was it them?

Abe's jaw did not drop and hit the floor, but he wished he were up in bed with his eyes closed. If he ever, ever got to Egypt, and he ever, ever met his aunts or cousins there, they would be bound to say: 'The path across the desert is never straight', because Abe's path to a fortune had twisted right into this changing room and disappeared. His miracle, miniature football team that would make him a millionaire had somehow become a gaggle of old men. He blinked. They blinked back. It was them. He knew it was them because they were all wearing football shorts and shirts, like in the photo.

He should have backed out of the room. He should have run upstairs and found matron and burst into tears and said he had been very frightened, not that that would have worked because he had tried it one time before. He should have run and told the headmaster that there were eleven strange men in the changing room. He should, at the very least, have quietly closed the door and gone back down the corridor and stood in front of another photograph.

But of course he didn't, and he couldn't. He pulled his dressing gown tight round him and re-knotted the cord.

'It's him! The boy outside!'

'Jimmy!'

'He could put us back.'

'Shut up.'

'I don't want to go back.'

They were all round him, pushing and shoving, some grinning, some worried, one rubbing his sleeve along his nose, and one, Abe registered, standing a little back from the others. Everything was so weird that all Abe could think was how come their clothes fitted because they were all so different: skinny, dumpy, big, gangly, balding, bearded . . . What a team! And who was Jimmy? And if they weren't quiet they would have Mrs Dunne scorching her way down the corridor and then there would be a few scalps hanging up as trophies, and Abe didn't want his to be one of them.

'Shshsh!'

There was a moment's pause in the babble and the man who'd been standing a little apart stepped forward. He was a tall, wiry chap, with thinning hair, and eyes that looked sleepily mischievous. 'Look what's crawled out of the woodwork, chaps, old Jungle Jim himself.'

'Sorry?'

And immediately the hubbub started up again.

They may have been around sixty years older than they had been in the photo, but they hadn't grown up. Any idiot could see that. They were shoving, and tripping, and some of them were asking him impossible questions about people he'd never heard of, and already they seemed to have forgotten what had happened to them.

'Yes, yes, of course, I'll do what I can . . . ' He backed his way out of the scrum. What could he do? In the photograph, the same age as him; now, their lives three quarters gone—pfssh! like that.

It was . . . unholy.

What was he going to do with them? Get them back in the photograph? How? And even if he could, was that fair? Find their homes? Where do you begin with eleven old men in football shorts! He needed help. He needed a magic word; he needed the power of the desert; the power of the Nile . . . even a halfway good idea would do. Meanwhile they needed him.

He saw the tall, thin man threading his way towards him. He seemed so familiar; that half smile. 'You are Griffin?' he asked as the man came up to him.

'That's me, Jimmy.'

'I'm not Jimmy.'

'Course you are: Jungle Jimmy.' The man gave his hands a brisk rub together. 'Now, how about sorting some tea and sambos?' He gave Abe a wink and then without waiting for his response he turned round to the team and said: 'Tucker?'

'Starving!' they all chorused.

He gave Abe another wink. 'There you are, old chap, you heard them. Hop to it. Pints of tea and lashings of sandwiches, cucumber, no crusts.' And with that Griffin turned his back on him and started to talk to a very round man whom he called Bink.

Tucker, lashing, sambos, Jimmy, cucumber, no crusts. Racist, rude, and who did they think they were? He had never liked being bossed around and he certainly didn't like being called Jimmy. He grabbed a hockey stick and gave Griffin a sharp jab in the back. Then, before Griffin could turn round, jumped up on a changing bench so that he would be looking down rather than up at him.

'What the—'

' . . . Dickens,' offered Abe. He had heard teachers use that expression.

'That hurt, you know,' complained Griffin. 'I thought you were going to help.'

'Did you?' Abe banged the bench with the stick so that the room fell silent and all eyes were on him and Griffin. Too bad if they were heard, they couldn't have made much more noise than they had already. 'Why should I help you, any of you?'

Griffin shrugged. 'You're the little chappie through the glass. You're always there.' He turned to the others. 'He was, wasn't he, always staring.' He pulled a dopey face and the others laughed. 'We got a bit fed up . . . '

'A bit fed up!' snapped Abe. 'You were behind glass. You were stuck. You were just a photograph until I released you. Do you realize that?' He underlined it for them. 'I released you.'

This caused a good bit of embarrassed shuffling.

'Thanks.'

'Damn decent.'

'How did you do it?'

'Some things,' said Abe with a deliberate air of mystery, 'I can do.' They looked impressed. 'Do you know where you are?'

'Prackton Hall.'

'Yes. Do you know when you are?'

'What's he mean?' asked a solid looking, mischievous-faced man, the goalkeeper—Jack.

Abe waited. The boys started to mutter to each other. Griffin looked at Roberts and Roberts, under his breath said, 'I'm really starving, can't he get us the tucker without the speech?' Griffin didn't answer.

'I mean,' said Abe, 'do you know what the date is, what year this is? Do you?'

'1942.' This was Griffin, but he wasn't looking quite so sure of himself.

'Is that what you think? Well, let me put you right. The date is 2002. You are in the next century. You have been in a photograph for sixty years.'

Complete silence.

Then an explosion as if they had been hit by a bad smell.

'Puwah!'

'Jerry hasn't bloody won the war, has he?' asked a very small man with a quavery voice. Stokely, thought Abe, back row second from left.

'Not if my dad's still flying Spitfires!'

'Listen! There are no Spitfires any more.'

'What!' Their turn to be outraged.

'Well, maybe one or two. The war is over. It's been over for years. Look at yourselves.'

They looked. They looked again, that is, and this time maybe some of what Abe had been trying to tell them registered.

Bink Roberts looked down at his stomach. 'It was never that large,' he said.

Griffin was gingerly touching his scalp. 'And I had hair.'

'Me too.'

'And you're all grey.'

'So are you.'

Abe watched them and felt sorry. One by one they fell silent and turned towards him.

'What are we going to do . . . er . . . Jimmy?' Griffin, his head cocked on one side, was eyeing him. 'Can't go back to school, can we?'

'No.'

'No more school, everybody!'

There was a complete, seismic change of mood: they shoved, poked, tweaked, kicked, and cheered. Abe waited. Gradually the delight faded as they remembered the strangeness of their situation.

'What are we going to do?' said Griffin. 'Can't stay here, can we? And we're hungry.'

'Could eat an elephant,' muttered Roberts.

'He got us out. He can get us home, can't he?' piped Stokely.

'Can you?'

Abe and Griffin looked at each other. 'I don't know,' Abe said. 'Maybe, but I know it's not safe for you here. And if I am going to help, you're going to have to do what I tell you.'

'We're a team. We do what we're told, don't we?'

Abe didn't trust him but he noticed the ones who nodded seriously—Stokely, Bittern, Chivers. There were also one or two who grinned and he heard a muttered, 'Mostly', from somewhere at the back.

They were going to be very hard work, that was for sure.

'If I am the one who let you out I am also,' Abe said, very slowly and very clearly, 'the one who can put you right back there.'

There was an uncomfortable murmuring. Someone in a hushed voice said: 'Magic.' Someone else said: 'Shush.'

Odd. Abe felt a tingle down the back of his scalp. Magic? He looked at them and all of them, including Griffin, looked nervously back at him. They knew something, something about what had happened to them, something, perhaps, that they would rather forget. Well, if it helped to keep them in order that was good, so once again he laid the threat before them: 'Yes, I can put you back, if that is what you want.'

'We'd rather you didn't.'

'Absolutely.'

'Do as we're told.'

'All right,' said Abe, 'I'll help you on two conditions: you call me Abe, not Jimmy or Jungle Jim or anything else. I am not your servant. Secondly, you do what I tell you.' They nodded. All of them this time. 'And there's no food till tomorrow morning. Too risky to go into the kitchens now. I am going to have to hide you somewhere until we can work out how to get you back,' he hesitated, 'to your families. We have to be very, very careful. If we're caught, it could be prison or, worse still, we could end up doing jobs for the headmaster's wife for the rest of our lives.'

It was the most horrible thing that Abe could think of but, as soon as he'd said it, he realized it probably meant nothing to them at all.

He couldn't have been more wrong.

THREE

They were stunned.
They were terrified.
They looked at each other.

Then Stokely collapsed on a bench and put his grey-haired head in his hands. 'I want to go home,' he said. 'I want to go home to Mummy.'

Nobody sneered. Nobody said anything until one of them, Abe thought it was Thomas, under his breath almost, muttered: 'The witch!' and exchanged a glance with the man beside him—Jonson, left wing, a gentle looking man with a shiny domed head.

Griffin looked appalled but portly Bink Roberts went completely white, and began to tremble violently; his eyes rolled upwards so you could only see the whites.

It looked terrifying.

'What's happening to him?' said Abe. 'Is it a heart attack?'

The team gawped like so many stationary goldfish. 'Help him, someone! Griffin!'

'Ug. Ug,' gurgled the fat forward and then, just as he began to keel over, threatening to whack his face into the bench, Abe leapt down from where he was standing and grabbed him. Unluckily for Abe, Roberts was too big, too heavy, and Abe was a fraction too late and so, with his arms stretched round Roberts's extensive middle, Abe toppled slowly backwards.

'Phheeeeuph!' Air burst out of Abe's lungs; his ribs pancaked and for a moment everything went black.

When he opened his eyes, he saw a ring of worried faces looking down at him and something black and shiny which turned out to be the top of Roberts's head.

'Bit of a crash landing,' was Griffin's helpful comment.

'Get him off me,' wheezed Abe, 'please.'

The accident seemed to have restored the team's spirits a little. At least they showed themselves capable of action and even of some concern. They rolled Roberts over so he landed with a bit of a thump on the floor, and hauled Abe upright. 'Does he do that often?' asked Abe.

'Oh no,' said Chivers, one of the serious ones: a tall man, a head taller than the others, with a slight stoop and an apologetic smile. 'Bink got a fright, that's all. It was what you said. It brought it all back, poor chap.'

'He'll be OK when he's had some tucker,' said Griffin.

'Brought all what back?'

A babble of voices started up.

'She did it. Don't you remember she was standing right behind the photographer and she had that horrible smile on her face.'

'She liked Roberts awfully, didn't she?'

'But she was such a squit.'

'Always looking at him.'

'Peeking through the changing room door, do you remember?'

'Beastly. And always sneaking to her beastly mother.'

'The head's wife! She was just as bad.'

'Ugh!'

And then in a kind of awed hushed voice first one and then another, then all of them said: 'She was a witch. Really she was. Her and her mother. Witch.'

'No, no, wait,' said Abe. 'Just slow down. You're all crowding around me and I can't think. I can hardly breathe.' He sat down on the bench and rubbed his eyes, while the team, a little creakily, squatted down on the floor around him. Here they were, the team from the photograph: 1942, and one of them out cold, whale-like, making little snorting noises through his nose.

Who was going to believe this? None of his friends upstairs, that was for sure, not his mother either. Mother? He thought of Mrs Dunne. Alicia was perfect, and normal of course, but Mrs Dunne—well, she was horrible enough to be a witch but she just didn't look like one: too headmistressy and no broomstick, no black cat, no transforming spells, just ordinary, run-of-the-mill, spiteful nastiness.

'What was the girl's name?'

'Deadly Delia. That's what we called her. She had round buggy eyes.'

'She made you feel funny when she stared,' said Jonson.

'Yes,' added Thomas, 'and she always seemed to be muttering to herself and waving her fingers around. We thought it was silly girls' games . . . '

But Abe was only half listening because he suddenly felt as if he had been plugged into the mains electricity. This was all sixty years ago. What was Mrs Dunne? Hard to tell. But here she was, the girl, now grown, hating boys . . . and what she had done to them was real magic—black magic, not something from a children's story, but real, and here were the boys whose lives she had stolen. But she didn't do anything like this now, did she? He couldn't think of any of his friends who'd suddenly disappeared or had had something terrible happen to them. Yet she was evil, no doubt about that, and she could have done such a thing. But why only that one time? Had she used up her power? Or perhaps her trapping the boys like that had been, what was the word, a fluke.

'Tell me again,' Abe said, 'and slowly, what you think happened.'

'It's not what we think, it's what we know,' said Griffin. The team earnestly nodded their heads in agreement, and then Griffin, with quite a few 'Isn't that right, chaps?' and 'We all saw that one coming, didn't we?', related how this strange little girl had developed an immense and quite inexplicable crush on poor old Bink who, despite being a jolly fine person and surprisingly fast on his feet, was absolutely terrified of girls generally and the headmaster's daughter in particular. No one else took the girl's crush on Bink as anything more than complete bonkersness—after all, she was only eight. But eventually Bink got really, really fed up so the team held a council of war and decided to play a trick on her. Bink left a note saying that she should meet him in the gym at midnight but when she crept down there, all alone in the dark, the team, who had hidden themselves behind all the equipment, the rolled up mats, stacked benches, and the vaulting horse, jumped out and spooked her. She ran off like a scalded cat, hair standing right up on end.

'You never saw anything like it,' said Jack. 'Jolly funny.' Stokely nudged him and told him to shut up. He did.

Abe, who was still puzzling over the meaning of 'bonkersness', didn't think it sounded funny at all. It was cruel. About as cruel and mean as Mrs Delia Dunne herself.

The next day, continued Griffin, there had been school and team photographs, and that was when it happened. She was standing behind the photographer watching him get ready and then when he ducked under his black cloth and just before he said 'Smile, boys', she took out her hankie and dabbed her eyes, pretending to cry. Then she gave a little wave and there was a big flash and the next thing they knew they were in the strange world behind glass, where time didn't seem to happen, and they never got hungry, apart from Bink, and they just were terribly, terribly bored. At first the girl used to come along and grin at them, and mouth things that they couldn't hear, but then she stopped coming and after that they never, ever saw anyone or anything until Abe appeared, always in the darkness of the evening. They thought he was a bit of a funny fellow, not being English and all that, so Griffin began the jokes just to cheer them all up.

And now they were old. Just like that, a snap of the fingers, thought Abe, and a lifetime disappears but the girl,

she, Mrs Dunne, she lived her life. She married . . .
'Who was the headmaster in 1942?' he asked suddenly.

'Kennet,' said Griffin, 'Commodore Kennet.'

'Retired naval officer?'

'Yes.'

'Funny.'

'Odd.'

'This one's a sailor too.'

Griffin looked blank.

'And Mrs Kennet?'

'Definitely peculiar. Like the girl, you know.'

Abe took a breath and glanced around at the team;
Jack, who looked every bit the overgrown practical joker,
was absent mindedly stuffing a pair of dirty football socks
down Bink Roberts's shirt. The rest were all waiting for
Abe to speak. 'The good news,' he said, 'is that Mrs
Kennet is not here; the bad news is that your girl, Delia, is
now my headmaster's wife.'

'No!'

'Is she bad?'

'Yes, of course.'

'Do people just do things when she looks at them?'

'Yes, but . . . '

'Crikey. She's like her mother. Mrs Kennet was like
that.'

The team moaned.

All of them apart from Thomas. He grabbed Abe by
the arm. 'But you got us out, didn't you now. You'll have
to think very clever. Think very foreign.'

'I'm half Egyptian.'

'Good. Great,' said Thomas eagerly. 'I'm Welsh, you
know. You'll have to think very Egyptian. Bound to do
the trick. Egypt. Moses.'

Jonson nodded. 'Frogs,' he said.

'Exactly,' said Thomas. 'Frogs. You know, that sort of
thing.'

'Please!'

'You have to.'

The babble started. The noise level climbed. Abe closed his eyes. This was going to be hard. Then, quite extraordinarily, with all the noise, and Thomas shaking his arm, he had a swift picture in his mind of dark skies, the Great Pyramid, and a wide, wide river. Perhaps I am the chosen one, he thought and then was instantly astonished at himself. What a peculiar thought. He opened his eyes and there was Thomas mouthing something at him.

'Moses was Egyptian, wasn't he?'

'No. No!' It was bedlam. Chosen? What did he mean 'chosen'? This was a nightmare. If he didn't keep a grip, didn't keep calm, he'd end up as strange as all these men in shorts. Be clever, he said to himself, be wise. He took a deep breath.

'I've said I'll help, so I will, but you must be quiet. You don't want her to hear you, do you?'

'Who,' asked a cool voice, 'is the *her*?'

A different voice.

Griffin put a knuckly finger to his lips and leaned back to peer round the end of the row of changing lockers, and then turned back to them. He pulled a sour face and mouthed: 'A girl.'

The vision! Before the team could faint, burst into tears, or start beating each other with games bags, Abe jumped up onto the bench. 'It's OK, it's fine,' he said to the team, and then: 'Hi. Brilliant. Alicia! What are you doing here?' It wasn't like her to wander about—her mother would spin into a tornado of black fury. But there she was, standing in the open doorway, hands clasped in front of her, head tilted on one side. If it weren't for her usual wonderfully startling dark lipstick and eye shadow, and the glinting stud in her nose, she would almost look girlish.

'I wondered what had happened to you, Nasfali,' she said. 'You weren't in your usual spot when I came out so I thought I ought to check. Wouldn't want Mummy to have done anything terrible to you.' She sounded businesslike. 'Who were you talking about, when you said "her"?'

Abe found himself tightening his dressing gown cord and smoothing his pyjama collar while at the same time thinking that her arrival was a stroke of good luck. She was exactly who they needed. She would know everything, wouldn't she? But would she help? She might. She had given him the old thumbs up.

'Nasfali, we're all waiting.'

'Your mother,' he said awkwardly. 'Thought she might get a bit cross.'

'You mean like thunder?'

'Like a tornado, actually.'

'Yes,' she agreed, 'very likely. She can certainly be like that.'

One by one the team, apart from poor Bink Roberts, were levering themselves up and either on to the bench or into a position where they could peer over the lockers. An odd sight for Alicia Dunne, perhaps, to have this row of aged heads with various expressions of surprise, fear, admiration even, peering at her over metal lockers, and between odd rugby shirts and shapeless games bags.

However, she ignored the team. 'You look a bit of a dummy, Nasfali,' she said, not unsympathetically.

'That's what I called him.' Griffin looked at the vision and then at Abe and nudged him in the ribs. 'Who is she?' he whispered. 'And why does she look so odd?'

Abe shook his head.

Her eyes shifted to Griffin. 'And who are you?'

'I'm Griffin,' said Griffin and then when she didn't respond, added lamely: 'The captain, you know.'

'You don't look like a captain.'

'I say . . . ' began Griffin, but she glanced at him and he clamped his mouth shut.

Alicia stepped inside the changing room, letting the door close behind her, and walked down to the end of the row where they all were. Ten heads followed her progress. When she saw the team, or rather when she saw what they were wearing, she burst into a snort of laughter. 'What have you done, Nasfali? I mean where *did* you find all these wrinklies?'

Abe didn't think this was fair. He hadn't done anything, not really, only take a photograph out of a frame and then put it back. 'From a photograph,' he said.

'Wicked!' she sounded impressed. 'There are only ten, shouldn't there be one more?'

The team parted to reveal the gently heaving mound that was Roberts.

'Tired, is he?'

Abe began to explain and Alicia, without any expression of surprise or disbelief, listened. 'Hm,' she said, eventually interrupting him when he got to the moment of the spell. 'Always thought there was something odd about that particular photograph. You'll have to tell me the rest later because we must hide them before Mummy gets here; she's on the prowl.'

'Oh no,' groaned Abe. 'What are we going to do?'

'Weren't you listening, Nasfali? I said hide them. Come on, think of something. I'm always hearing your name, Nasfali. Mother doesn't like you, you know.'

Of course he knew that.

'Doesn't like any boys really.'

The team looked glum.

'Or men for that matter, not even Daddy, I expect. Well?'

The sudden question startled Abe. 'Well, what?'

'You're not thinking,' said Alicia.

There was silence.

He thought.

And then he looked up. Twelve pairs of eyes, Roberts having come to in the meantime, were studying him with interest. 'Well,' he said, 'it won't be very comfortable, but the shooting range isn't being used at the moment, and if we can sort out food . . . '

'And some clothes,' said Alicia studying the assortment of knobbly knees, gangly elbows, and a few round bellies straining under the old-fashioned white football shirts.

'Then,' said Abe, 'tomorrow it's Sports Day and there will be loads of people around, and maybe we can slip them out of the school. Then . . . '

' . . . think what to do.' There was, for the first time, a hint of a smile on Alicia's face. 'You're doing all right so far,' she said.

'Do you mean, you're going to help me?'

'Don't start getting ideas,' said the vision.

'But I thought that's what you wanted.'

'Goodnight,' she said. 'You can sort them out tonight. I'll meet you at six thirty down at the kitchen.'

'But breakfast isn't till seven thirty.'

'Exactly.' And with that Alicia Dunne slipped back out into the dark corridor and Abe was left with his team.

'No complaints,' he said quickly. 'And no noise.'

To his surprise he had them quiet and lined up in no time at all. They knew where the shooting range was and, their high spirits having evaporated, would probably have trooped quietly over there on their own, but Abe wasn't sure whether it was unlocked and he couldn't remember whether there was a light down there. So he led the way, left out of the changing room, through the boot-room, out into the yard, across the cricket pitch and then down some steps by the pavilion. There it was: half underground and probably full of spiders.

He pushed the door; it swung open. He fumbled to the right and found the light switch. He turned it on. A feeble bulb glowed dully from the middle of the stone ceiling and he ushered them in.

'There,' said Abe. 'Not that bad.' In fact it was Abe's least favourite place in the school. The room was small with wooden benches round the wall. There were two bristly mats on the floor in front of the two tunnels. You lay on the mat. The teacher in charge sneered at you, and you then shot down the tunnel at a target that always seemed to go blurred when Abe looked at it.

The team sat down on the benches.

'Well,' said Abe, 'I'd better get back before anyone notices I've gone.'

'Thanks for the rescue,' said Roberts glumly.

'Yes,' they chorused. 'Thanks awfully.'

'I'll . . . em . . . try and sort out some food in the morning.' Abe pulled the door behind him and, just for a moment, waited but heard nothing and so set off back across the cricket pitch. They must be worn out, he thought. Being a picture on the wall one minute and an old-age pensioner the next . . . He shuddered. And being old, just like that: old hands, and white stubble on your face. How could you do that to someone? Steal half their life. It was a terrible thing, and there was no profit in it. Not that he could see, and not that that would make it right, of course.

It was so still. The moon was clear, and the main building of Prackton Hall was dusted with cool, silvery light that made it seem taller, and thinner, and the windows like blind eyes, gazing down at him. He shivered, though it was a mild night. He glimpsed a shape drift over the roof, and an owl screeched, then from back across the pitch he heard the sound of stifled laughter. Surely they couldn't be up to something; they looked far too miserable, all of them. Should he go back? He hesitated but then he saw the last lights up at the top of the building blinking off. The senior dormitory. He'd have to run or someone would notice he wasn't in bed.

Once inside the main building he eased open the door to the corridor. The single light was still on, so the headmaster hadn't come back to check on him. That was good. He took the stairs two at a time, and poked his head into the matron's room where the green bottle was out on the table, but there was no sign of Miss Chirt.

Good.

He made it to the room he shared with six other boys, and slipped into his bed. 'OK, Abe?' asked a sleepy voice. 'Thought you'd be left down there all night.'

'Yes, Droid, I am all right, thank you.'

'Good.'

'Droid?' but his friend was already asleep. He wondered whether he should wake him, and the others too perhaps; but he didn't. Another week, that was all, and then holidays for them, trips abroad, houses in the country for some, brothers and sisters and cousins and then senior school. Their lives were sorted. For him: that boring, polished apartment in London; his ice-cool mother, and only the big plan, the grand scheme to get to Cairo, to keep him going.

The doorway darkened. 'Nasfali!' The voice was as soft as rotten fruit: Alicia's mother. 'Why is your light on?'

'I'm so sorry, Mrs Dunne, I was tired from standing downstairs, I . . . I . . . '—a bit of a stutter was always good for effect—'must have fallen asleep.'

'Did you report to matron?'

'She wasn't in her room. I just saw a strange green bottle. It looked like alcohol, Mrs Dunne, and I thought I oughtn't to wait in case Miss Chirt was perhaps a bit . . . ' he let his voice trail away.

'Nonsense! That's medicine.' Mrs Dunne snapped the door to without even waiting for Abe to turn off his light.

If that's medicine, then you, Mrs Dunne, are a one-legged goat. Abe smiled. Maybe the evening wasn't so bad. A few problems, perhaps, he thought sleepily, but if Alicia managed to get clothes for the team, they could mingle them with the parents who'd be all over the place tomorrow and as long as they behaved themselves, the team could easily pass off as fathers. Then what? There would be hundreds of cars parked all over the front field but that wasn't any good. They couldn't all drive off in different cars, and anyway, he supposed, none of them could drive.

Abe rolled over on to his side so that he could see the moon through their curtainless window. It was like a single headlight. Or a flat coin. Heads or tails? What they really needed, he decided, before gently sliding off to sleep, was a coach. Yes, a coach for the team.

FOUR

Abe woke up, stretched and stared at the ceiling. Saturday. Sports Day. Strawberries and cream. He smiled. Oh yes! And the races. Abe had a high opinion of his skill as an athlete. I am very fast over short distances, he thought smugly. Very fast. He rolled on his side and admired the little pyramid clock he had made for himself in Tech. Creamy yellow. Sands of the great desert. The minute hand clicked. Six twenty-nine.

Time.

Team! 1942! He squawked. Then rammed his face into the pillow to stop himself squawking again.

His friend, Droid, stirred and someone else murmured: 'Chicken?'

Abe pulled the pillow from his face. How could he have forgotten? He was late. He sat up and swung his legs out of bed. Should he wake the others? But even as he asked himself the question he knew he wouldn't. They never believed the stories he made up about his secret family in Cairo so why should they believe this? He, Ebrahim Nasfali, hardly believed it, and yet it was true. He took a deep breath in through his nose and then stretched out his arms. I am chosen, he thought, and that pleased him. He didn't often feel chosen.

And she, Alicia, was she chosen too?

Abe offered up a quick prayer. Then shoved his clothes on over his pyjamas, looked at his toothbrush, then crept to the door and peered out. All clear. He would talk to her. She said she would be there, in the kitchen, but would she? And if she was there, would she help? Would she help even if her mother had terrible powers and could trap living people, boys, like himself, in a photograph?

Chosen or not, Abe, for perhaps the first time in his life, was not convinced that he could cope on his own.

Oh, Alicia Dunne, please be chosen, he prayed, as he sped along the passage, down the stairs, past matron's room and arrived two minutes later, out of breath, in the kitchen.

Alicia Dunne, wearing a pale pink dress, white socks, and heavy black boots, was already there, standing over the stove, putting egg after egg into a huge, steaming saucepan. She glanced at him coolly. 'Your pyjamas are showing,' she said, 'and you're late.'

'Oh.' Why was it that, glorious as she was, when she spoke to him he felt as if he were in the eye of a storm. The words *he* wanted to say were snatched away from him. 'Big wind,' was all he managed.

'What?'

'You are like a great wind of the desert.' That was better.

'Really?' Her eyes creased slightly. It might have been a smile. 'Three minutes or four for boiled eggs?' she said. 'Boiled eggs are a disgusting habit but that's exactly the sort of things boys eat.'

'I like yogurt, strong cheese, and meat.'

'That's also disgusting. How long for the eggs?'

'I don't know. It doesn't really matter, does it?'

'No.' She eyed him. 'What are you waiting for?'

'What?'

'The team. Go and get them.'

Abe paused at the door. 'You look very nice,' he said.

'Nice,' she sniffed and poked at the simmering eggs.

Nice? Why did he say nice? He could have said something fine, something elegant: 'You are like the silver moon . . . ' No. 'You are magnificent, blinding like the desert sun.' Certainly not. 'You are winding and wiggly like the great Nile.'

No, that wouldn't do at all. He pushed open the door to the shooting range. The trouble was she wasn't really like anything else; she was just . . .

'Not here!'

It didn't take a genius to see instantly that the place was deserted: there was the bristle mat, the bare benches, the two shooting range tunnels, which he checked, brushing the dirt and cobwebs from his hands as he did so. Nobody had spent the night there, that was for sure.

A small spider dangled from a thread.

Perhaps Mrs Dunne had found them? Perhaps they were back in 1942. What was Alicia going to say? Eleven boiled eggs.

He backed out, closed the door, and then looked across the pitch to the school. Still, no one around? No. Good. He bounded up the steps and was already running when he heard sharp yapping. The headmaster's dog, a terrier, had emerged from the bushes at the edge of the field at exactly the same moment as Abe had come up the steps and had spotted him. It was a dog given to chasing anything that moved: cars, bikes, other dogs, in fact any living thing, which is why the headmaster exercised it early, before the school was awake, and then kept it locked up in his apartment where it hurled itself at the door if anybody passed by outside. Abe had forgotten about the dog. 'Give me, in my heels,' he now prayed, 'the speed of lightning.' But when he glanced over his shoulder, the wiry terrier with its keen interest in biting anything that moved was gaining on him.

One hundred metres. His legs pumped and his arms punched and he ran as hard and as fast as he had ever run. But the dog was concentrating equally hard. It had stopped yapping and had got so close that Abe could hear the disgusting panting sound it was making. He imagined its teeth sinking into his calf and then he was spinning round the corner of the art room, and there were just a couple of yards to the school's back door. Instinct made him dart back, out of the way, against the wall, and as he did so he saw the terrier, its spiky teeth bared, momentarily airborne, and then, having miscalculated, landing in the dog equivalent of a forward roll. Abe took the opportunity to leap over the stunned animal, and slam through the door.

He leant against the closed door and took a breath. Safe, for the moment anyway. On the other side of the door, he could hear the little terrier scratching and whining. 'Oh, just go away,' he said. 'Leave me alone!' To his surprise, the dog gave an answering yap, and then there was silence. Coincidence?

Never.

He pressed his ear to the door. The headmaster? No. Someone else was outside. The dog gave a sudden yelp as if its ear had been yanked, and a razor thin voice said: 'You pointless creature! Where is she? I know she's done something.' Another yelp. 'Find her.'

Abe held his breath and stayed with his back pressed to the door. What was Mrs Dunne up to, patrolling the grounds at this hour in the morning? His stomach tightened into a hard, gripey knot; only the thin wood of the door between him and Alicia's mother, and if she found him he would be kebabed. He heard the slight sound of the dog's nails clicking unevenly on the path as it limped off, and then a long, deep sniff, not as if Mrs Dunne were suffering from a cold, but purposeful as if she were trying to scent something—or someone.

He tiptoed from the door, through the boot-room and into the corridor, then sprinted to the changing room, giving it a quick check to see if the team had slunk back there for some reason, and then along the corridor again, lifting 1942 from the wall as he passed, and burst round the corner and into the kitchen. 'They've gone!'

'Why've you got that?' She pointed with a spoon to the photograph he was clutching in his hands.

'To see if they're in it again.'

'Are they?'

He looked. A little bit of ground, and an empty bench. 'No.'

'Then they're somewhere in the school. Or,' she pulled a face, 'mother has found them.' She scooped the last of the boiled eggs out of the pot and added it to the row she had marching down the middle of the table.

'I don't think so.' And Abe told her how he had heard Mrs Dunne with the dog. 'It's you she's after but she doesn't know what you've done.'

'Me?' She gave a little smile to herself. 'What could I possibly do to upset my dear mother?'

'I don't know,' said Abe.

'Of course you don't.' She paused. He wished he wasn't wearing his pyjamas under his trousers. She was bound to comment on it again. But what she said was: 'You know she hates that dog almost as much as she hates boys. Give me the photograph.' He handed it over and she placed it face down, without even glancing at it. 'I'll look after it, I think. Now, if mother doesn't have the team, she probably doesn't even know they're missing. That is very interesting, isn't it?' Abe couldn't see why but said nothing. 'Well, they're somewhere in the school. Think, Nasfali, and be quick.' She raised a pierced eyebrow. 'Go.'

He went. Should she be telling him what to do all the time? And she was enjoying herself, he could see that. Was it some sort of game, she and her mother? If so, it was a dangerous game; not for Alicia perhaps, but for him it was, and the team.

Where could they be? Where would he go, if he had been told to spend the night in the shooting range? Where would he go? Somewhere with beds, of course. And where do you find empty beds in a school?

He was already running up the stairs. The infirmary: it was up on the floor above the dormitories, and isolated from the rest of the school.

From the outside, Prackton Hall was a large, imposing building; inside, however, much of it was a tangle of odd little rooms threaded together by narrow passages that disappeared round unlit corners and up twisting stairwells. Though out of bounds, Abe knew his way around the upper floors and so was able to speed unhesitatingly through the west wing and up two half-flights of stairs to the infirmary.

And that's where they were. He could hear the snoring and grunting before he reached the top of the stairs. 'There is no doubt about it, Ebrahim,' he said to himself, 'you are a genius.' Then, he twisted the door knob and peeked in.

As there were only six beds in the room, the team had pushed them all together, and were sleeping in a kind of nest of thin blankets and pillows, all arms and legs in such a tangle it was hard to tell one from the other. They reminded him of a litter of piglets; rather large and slightly ancient piglets.

He hustled them and shook them, pulled off sheets, and finally bullied them all awake enough to realize that food was a strong possibility. 'Tucker,' they muttered to each other, pulling on their shoes.

Abe spotted Griffin. 'I hid you all in the shooting range, and then you go and sneak up here. What if you'd been spotted? What if I hadn't found you? There's only half an hour before the whole school is up, you know.'

Griffin ducked his head. 'Sorry,' he said, though he didn't sound too penitent. 'It's just that the shooting range was a terrible idea.' Then he jabbed the old boy next to him who'd muttered something that Abe couldn't catch. 'Shut up, Jonson, you smell of old rats.' At this they began to giggle and to jostle each other. A pair of rolled up games socks looped up into the air and bipped Abe on his forehead.

'Shsh!' said Abe. They were making too much noise. 'Shsh!' They ignored him. How he would have hated to be a teacher, standing up in front of a class, hissing and shushing like a steam engine. No, he certainly didn't have the patience.

He stepped over to Griffin, poked a finger in his skinny chest. 'Mrs Dunne is looking for you and unless you shut up, she'll find you. Since I don't want her to find me, I'm off.' Griffin looked at him a bit startled and as the sense of what he was saying filtered through the giggles of the rest of the old boys, they gradually fell silent. 'If you want her to do something horrible to you, please stay here; if you want breakfast, you come with me now, and quietly.'

'Sorry,' said Griffin. He turned to the others. 'What do you say?'

'Very sorry. It won't happen again.'

They sounded genuine, though when Abe turned to open the door he was sure he heard one of them suppress a splutter, but he ignored it. 'Single file.'

They creaked past the silent dormitories, and down a narrow staircase that took them down right to the kitchen, where Alicia was sitting at the head of the table sipping a cup of thick black coffee. She raised a ring-pierced eyebrow. 'Come and sit down, boys,' she said and, surprisingly meekly, they took their places on either side of the table, heads all turned towards her. 'You can start,' she said.

Instantly a feeding frenzy took over, elbows and hands pumped up and down, and spoons of cereal were sloshed into hungry mouths. Well, they haven't eaten for sixty years, thought Abe.

Alicia snapped her fingers. 'Toast please, Nasfali.'

Before he knew what he was doing, he was scuttling to and from the huge smoking ten-at-a-time toaster, trying not to burn his fingers. The row of boiled eggs was whittled away one at a time and, oddly, it made Abe think about the team and how difficult it was going to be, first to keep them all together and then to find homes for them all.

Was this an adventure? He looked at the bowed thinning heads, shovelling egg into munching mouths. It didn't quite have the romance, notwithstanding Alicia in pink, of riding camels across the desert. Instead it seemed to have a great deal of rushing, and too many practical problems.

He slapped the last mound of toast on to the table and then slumped down on to a stool beside Alicia. Something wasn't right. There were two boiled eggs left in the middle of the table. 'You cooked thirteen eggs,' he said.

'Did I?'

'Yes, why did you do that?'

'Extras,' she said brightly.

'Oh.'

'And it's my lucky number.' Abe frowned and she laughed. 'Three minutes to tidy up time,' she said looking at her watch.

'What are we going to do with them?' said Abe. 'Any time I ask them to do something they just snort and giggle. It's hopeless.'

'They're all right,' she said. 'Look.' And then she addressed the old boys. 'Two minutes left. The kitchen has to be spotless.'

There was a sudden clatter of knives and spoons and scraping of chairs and, quick as a flash, they were at the sinks, washing and drying and wiping the table.

'How did you do that?'

Alicia shrugged and finished the last of her coffee and then leaned back so that Stokely could pick up her cup and saucer. 'Thank you,' she said. Stokely blushed and hurried back to the sink. Abe noticed how her eyes followed him and then roved over all of them, watching them, smiling slightly.

'Why are you doing this?' said Abe. 'Why are you helping? Your mother will kill you if she finds out.'

Of course he didn't mean it literally but she looked at him as if he had. 'Oh, she won't kill me,' she said. 'She couldn't do that, but we'll have to be careful about you and the others.'

'Yes.' Abe had every intention of being very careful. He swallowed nervously.

'So that's why I'm helping, of course. To make up for her. My mother is so bad really. And anyway,' she added, 'this is fun.' She clapped her hands together. 'One minute left.'

There was a frantic flurry of cloths and wiping and drying and cutlery clashing into baskets. Abe stood up and pushed his stool under the table. 'You'll help me get them out of the school?'

'Yes, but,' she hesitated, as if making a calculation, 'I think we ought to do it today if we can. I have a feeling mother has something on this evening which could be wicked.'

'Wicked as in good?'

She shook her head. 'Wouldn't say so particularly.'

She clearly wasn't going to tell him more so he puffed out his cheeks and blew. 'Sports day. It's probably our best chance, but how?'

'You'll think of something.'

At that moment the team had completed their tidy up and automatically gathered round Abe and Alicia, who remained casually sitting down and studying her purple nail varnish.

'Well?' said Griffin.

Abe said: 'What we need to do is to—'

'Get you away from my mother,' interrupted Alicia. 'Or,' she said, scooping up the frame from beside her chair and showing it to them, 'she'll pop you into this photograph again before you can say skinnymalink.'

'Oh no,' said Griffin. 'Please, we don't want that.' The others murmured their unhappy agreement.

'Of course you don't,' said Alicia. 'So you're going to come with me and I'll find you some clothes, isn't that right, Nasfali?'

'Yes, of course. Then when the guests come for the sports you can mingle . . . '

'And Nasfali here will arrange transport so that we can get you safely away.'

'Where will you take us to?' asked Thomas. 'Because I think we'd all like to go home, really, if you don't mind.'

'If you don't mind,' echoed Jonson.

'Yes,' said Alicia briskly, 'but first things first. Now, all of you come with me. Nasfali, you had better make an appearance at breakfast or you'll get into trouble. We'll meet you in the marquee after the races. You are running, aren't you?'

'The marquee might be risky—strawberries and cream and them.'

Roberts nodded and Gannet licked his lips.

'They'll be fine,' said Alicia. 'They'll behave just like all the other awful parents. Won't you, boys?'

'Oh yes,' they agreed, though Abe felt they would automatically agree to anything Alicia said. Still, it did make sense—a gang of old men wandering around the grounds would be highly suspicious. Inside the big tent with everyone else, who would notice them, so long as they weren't in their football gear? 'OK,' he said. 'Can you get me a guest list?'

'Why?'

'Might be helpful.'

'I expect so.' And she sailed out, the photograph tucked under her arm and the team clustering in close after her.

Abe pulled a face then glanced round the kitchen. It looked all right. Then, before he could move, the outside door was pushed open and there with a sudden sharp reek of sweat and boiled cabbage was the barrel-chested chef, Lakin. 'Boy?' he rumbled sourly and licked his fat lips.

FIVE

Only ever glimpsed by the boys as they passed by the kitchen, the chef, Lakin, was not a pleasant sight: his large stomach wobbled tightly against his stained white shirt while his little, black pig eyes, wedged deep into his sweaty face, fastened on Abe.

'What's boy doin' in kitchen?' The way he spoke was somehow spitty, as if his tongue were too big for his mouth; and as he waddled, surprisingly quickly, from the door to the long table where the team had breakfasted and where Abe was still standing, he reached, without once taking his pig eyes from Abe, for a large wooden ladle hanging from his work top.

Abe was panicking. He couldn't move and he couldn't think. He was racking his brain for a decent excuse as to why he might be in Lakin's kitchen but nothing came to him, nothing that made any sense. 'Jam!' he blurted suddenly. 'No, no, toast . . . toast and milk.'

Lakin sidled round the table. Maybe it was that thick, rank smell closing in on Abe that finally jolted him into movement, because he took a step back. 'Whuddya mean, Jam-boy?' Lakin pointed a stubby finger at Abe and then crooked it, beckoning him. 'Come 'ere, Jam-boy.' And he rasped the ladle up and down his thigh, scratching himself.

Little bubbles of spit swelled, popped, and reappeared in the corner of the chef's mouth and Abe watched in horrid fascination. 'For the dog,' he somehow managed to say. 'Headmaster's dog. Had an accident. Told me, the headmaster told me to get the toast. A treat for it . . . ' He took another step back. The door to the corridor was, he reckoned, about five paces behind him and slightly to the right and his only hope was to make a dash for it and try to make it back to the dormitory before the morning bell rang. Droid and the others would automatically swear, if questioned, that he hadn't got up early. Oh, to be somewhere safe.

'Mrs Dunne said—'

'Mrs Dunne said I could deal with any boy that came into my kitchen, Jam-boy. Tha's wha' Mrs Dunne said.' Scratch went the ladle against his leg and his fat lips pulled back as he smiled horribly at Abe.

'No! Mrs Dunne said . . . Oh no!' and Abe suddenly shrieked and pointed wildly at the window behind Lakin. 'She's there!' The oldest trick in the book perhaps but in the split second that Lakin took his eyes off Abe, Abe turned and ran blindly for the door, wrenched it open and butted Mrs Dunne in the chest.

Lakin behind him, and Mrs Dunne in front; it was a nightmare sandwich.

Fingers hard as crab claws pinched both his ears. 'Nasfali,' pulling his head back and away from her, 'how fortunate. I think you called me?'

'No, Mrs Dunne, no, not really . . . ' The claws gave a sudden twist . . . 'Ow!'

'Oh yes, I think so,' she said and then: 'That will do, Lakin. Start the breakfast.'

'But you said,' spittled Lakin, 'I could deal with—'

'That will do, Lakin!'

Abe heard the heavy chef back off, grumbling to himself, and then the clatter of pans as he began his work. Mrs Dunne released his ears and while he gingerly fingered them to see whether they were still fully attached to the side of his head, she studied him, her face devoid of expression. 'Where is 1942, Nasfali?' she said.

Years of practice enabled Abe to look both surprised and innocent, though in fact he had felt a strong impulse to blurt out that Alicia had the photograph. '1942,' he said. 'I don't know what you mean . . . '

'You do, Nasfali,' her voice, for the first time, carrying

a hint of irritation. 'The photograph that is always right in front of you when you are made to stand in the corridor for punishment, Nasfali, and you are always being punished, Nasfali, because you are such a sly and horrible thief, and you have no doubt stolen that photograph for one of your money-making schemes. And I want it.'

'No, Mrs Dunne, really.' He thought of the way that the terrier had yelped before slinking off and he almost felt sorry for it.

'Would you like me to tell your mother that you are a thief?'

Abe didn't think his mother would care greatly what he was so long as it didn't cause her any bother. He shrugged.

'Did you know that we talk about you, Nasfali, your mother and me?'

'What?' That really did surprise him.

'Oh yes. She said that if you were any trouble at all, she would willingly pay to have you stay with us over the summer holidays. How would you like that, Nasfali?'

Prackton Hall on his own with just the Dunne family telling him what to do. It would be a wilderness, a stony desert. It would be suffering . . . But if Alicia were there . . .

Mrs Dunne's eyes narrowed. 'My daughter won't be spending the summer here.' Abe kept his face blank. 'Have you seen my daughter?'

'No.'

'Are you sure?'

'Yes.'

'She has spoken to you, hasn't she?' She sniffed. He remembered the way she had seemed to scent the air when he had been hiding behind the door to the boot-room. She caught his eye and he found himself desperately having to resist a desire to tell her everything. Words bubbled and danced on to the back of his tongue and threatened to spill out into the air of their own accord. He pretended to stifle a yawn, shoving his fist into his mouth. 'Hasn't she?' repeated Mrs Dunne.

Behind him, Abe could hear Lakin grumbling and muttering, the snap of rubber against skin and then the rasp of a knife being sharpened. Mrs Dunne's eyes flickered from Abe to the corner of the kitchen where Lakin worked and in that instant her hold on Abe slipped.

'No,' said Abe firmly, 'she hasn't.' He concentrated on Mrs Dunne's left shoulder and in doing so found that he no longer had such a strong desire to reveal the truth.

Mrs Dunne suddenly leaned towards him, sniffed again and, startled, Abe stepped back, but she gripped him by the chin and tilted his head up towards her. Then, with eyes half closed she began to sniff his face. Petrified, he couldn't move, trapped like a rabbit caught in the glare of a floodlight, or some small, insignificant desert creature hypnotized by the swaying dance of a snake. This was a new Mrs Dunne, not merely an unpleasant Mrs Dunne, but a dangerous Mrs Dunne; not a Mrs Dunne who, if the strange team of elderly boys were telling the truth, had done something uncanny and witch-like some sixty years before, but a Mrs Dunne standing right in front of him, her face inches from his, sniffing at him in a way that was not human.

The kitchen air was thick and heavy. It was difficult to breathe. It was also difficult to think: a rattle of images from the past night scattered like a deck of cards across his mind. There was no order to them, no beginning, no end: the corridor, Griffin's face, the shooting range, a spider, the photograph, Alicia . . .

Mrs Dunne began to smile, her mouth stretching, the tip of her pink tongue peeping between her teeth. At this moment she looked so different from the polished, attractive, and, yes, caring, headmaster's wife that parents so loved. She looked mad.

'I could make him squeal for you, Mrs Dunne.' The chef's mossy voice suddenly broke through Abe's semi-trance and Griffin's face faded like the Cheshire Cat's smile.

'Back to the stove, worm, and never, do you hear, never interrupt me again, if you value your loathsome life,' snarled Mrs Dunne. 'And as for you, Nasfali,' she said, releasing his chin with a little twist, 'thank you so much for telling me about my daughter and the boys in that photograph . . . ' and she took a deep breath so that her whole frame shuddered slightly.

'I didn't say anything.'

Mrs Dunne touched the fine gold chain she wore round her neck, blinked and then, once more respectable, said: 'You didn't need to, my dear.'

Abe swallowed. She had stolen into his mind, like a thief, peered and pried and poked around, hoping to find what she wanted. Had she though? His thoughts had been such a muddle, how much had she really discovered? Perhaps not everything, but she did seem to know about Alicia and the photograph. He must warn her. 'Can I go now, Mrs Dunne? I'm very sorry I was in the kitchen.'

She ignored his request. 'As for your punishment, Nasfali, let me see. I could let you run a few errands for Mr Lakin.' Abe involuntarily jerked around, fearing the chef might have sidled crab-like up behind him; but Lakin, his fat hands encased in surgical gloves, was in his corner, glowering as he smashed eggs and plopped the gooey yolk into a huge saucepan. 'Or,' continued Mrs Dunne, her tone brisk and businesslike, 'we could do with some help in the laundry room. Very hot in there and there are always so many dirty socks . . . '

'Of course,' said Abe.

'Meaning?' said Mrs Dunne. 'Meaning that you know how many socks there are? Meaning that you would love to be buried up to your neck in foul boys' socks? Is that what you mean, Nasfali?'

Abe had faced difficult situations before. His mother was difficult; school, particularly when you are bent on finding ways of making money, was difficult but it had never actually been dangerous. Mrs Dunne, however, was dangerous. Lakin was dangerous. He was not, he realized, involved in a splendid adventure where he might risk a nip from a terrier but had moved into much darker territory. It was time he proved once again that he could not only run extraordinarily quickly over short distances, but that he could think quickly too.

Not even Mrs Dunne would allow one of her students to be boiled, fried, or minced by Lakin, but the laundry room was a real threat; locked away in that sweaty little oven beside Miss Chirt's room, he would never have any chance to plan the next stage of their escape with Alicia, an escape for which they, of course, needed a coach or minibus. A bulb flickered in Abe's head.

Car park! Volunteers were always needed to guide parents on to the front field. Normally it was the responsible but not very sporty boys who landed this chore, but today he, Ebrahim Nasfali would be the master of cars. It might be a golden opportunity to solve their transport problem. 'Of course,' he said, in as beaten and as submissive a voice as he could manage, 'I am running in the one hundred metres and everyone expects me to win and if I did the laundry room I could be finished in time to race, so I really don't mind having that as a punishment, especially since boys' socks don't really smell that bad.'

Mrs Dunne's blonde eyebrows arched in surprise.

'But please,' continued Abe, 'whatever you do, don't make me do car parking; it goes on for ever and I just wouldn't be any good at it, and you know how the headmaster has a fit if the rows aren't straight and—'

'—He'll undoubtedly beat the living daylights out of you,' supplied Mrs Dunne with a sympathetic smile. In the background, Lakin offered an approving grunt. 'One of his sillier expressions. Well, off you go, Nasfali, report to my husband. He'll be delighted that you've volunteered.'

'Oh, Mrs Dunne, do I really have to?' Abe suppressed a smile. She wasn't that clever, after all.

'Off you go,' she said.

Abe bowed his head and dragged his heels to the door.

'Oh, Nasfali.'

'Yes, Mrs Dunne.'

'Thank you for telling me that Alicia has that photograph. I shall go and retrieve it instantly. It wouldn't do to have a blank spot on the wall, would it? I can't think what she's playing at. I might have been forced to hang someone up in its place. How would you like to be photographed, Nasfali?' and she laughed, a warm, pleasant laugh; the sound of someone enjoying herself.

The hairs on the back of Abe's neck bristled; that was an open threat. She clearly no longer cared that he knew her for what she was—an evil, boy-loathing witch. Who would believe him, or Alicia, or a bunch of elderly men in football shorts? He hurried out of her sight. She would do it, too, trap him behind glass and he would hang there, staring out on to that dim corridor and have unfortunate boys swinging from the radiator and staring back at him, having no idea that he was alive, ageing but not living.

He wondered whether he could warn Alicia before her mother got to her. He skipped up the back stairs to the first floor, turned right, pushed through a door covered in green baize and was then in the headmaster's domain. The corridor became a landing, overlooking the front hall. At the end of the landing a door led the way into the Dunne apartment where Alicia might be. It would be worth knocking on the door to find out; Mrs Dunne was out of the way. The only problem was that he had to pass by the headmaster's study in order to get to the end of the landing and although the headmaster should have been downstairs overseeing breakfast, he was in fact standing in front of a full length mirror, wearing what he called his 'sea rig', his captain's dress uniform which he always put on for school occasions, and knotting his tie, so he had a very clear view of Abe tiptoeing as stealthily and as delicately as a desert rat across his open doorway.

'Nasfali!' he boomed. 'What the devil are you doing up here? Come in here, you little sneaky person.'

'Oh, I was looking for you, sir.'

'Then what do you mean by going about on your tiptoes and why did you go creeping past my door?'

'Thought your family might be asleep. I didn't want to disturb them and then when I saw you . . . er . . . dressing in your very splendid uniform I thought it would be improper to intrude.'

'You are a very odd chap, Nasfali. Anyone tell you that? You don't talk like the other boys at all.'

'Yes, sir. Mrs Dunne told me I had to do car parking duty and to report to you.'

'Did she now? And did she know you were running in the hundred metres, eh?'

'I would think so.'

'Think so. Bad luck, then, Nasfali. Better not cross Mrs Dunne. Hang on a tick.'

Abe leaned against the wall outside his study. As he did so, the apartment door slowly eased open and Alicia's face appeared. 'Car park,' mouthed Abe.

She nodded. 'Have you eaten anything?' she mouthed back.

He shook his head. 'I think your mother knows.'

'What?' She pulled a face.

'Your mother.'

She appeared to be jostled by someone Abe couldn't see. 'Get back,' she hissed to whoever it was and then to Abe she mouthed: 'I have the list. I'll bring it down to you.'

And even as Abe was about to mouth 'mother' for the third time, she closed the door.

'Talking to yourself again, Nasfali,' said the headmaster. 'You really are a whatsit, aren't you. Follow me.'

He led Abe down the main stairs, collected a sheaf of red poles and then walked him round the front field, showing him where to place the poles as markers for the rows of cars. He gave Abe a white coat. 'Someone looking after you should be wearing one of these. Never mind, eh, stand by the gate and any problems just sort them out. I'll send a relief party before your race.' And he was off, steaming towards the playing fields.

As soon as he was out of sight, Alicia appeared with a sandwich and the guest list. 'No yogurt and strong cheese, I'm glad to say.'

Abe studied the list and absent-mindedly took a bite of the sandwich. 'Goat's cheese,' he said, surprised by the sharp taste.

'Yes,' she said, 'I was joking,' her expression as always completely serious. 'It's disgusting, isn't it.'

Abe smiled. 'I don't see anything useful here. Army people, navy people, people with long names. No good at all unless they come on a coach.'

'Turn over,' she said.

He turned over. Odd, he thought, he'd only noticed writing on one side when she had handed him the paper; but there, handwritten in a neat script, clearly visible in crimson ink, was the following information: 'Special provision: coach for guests of DD.'

'Your mum?'

'Yes.'

'What kind of special guests would she have?'

'Not very nice ones, I expect. You don't seem very pleased that we've now found a coach for the escape.'

'I am,' said Abe, 'but how are we, um, going to acquire possession?'

'You mean steal.'

'In a way,' said Abe, 'yes.'

52

'We'll think of something,' said Alicia dismissively. 'As soon as it turns up, come and find us in the marquee.'

He watched her run off, a little bit clumpily in her black boots, waving as she ran. He took another bite of his goat's cheese sandwich and for a moment thought he was in paradise.

An impatient hoot made him turn. An elderly lady mouthed at him through the closed window of her car. 'Can't hear a word, madam,' he said, trying not to spray bread and cheese at her. 'Park wherever you like,' and he waved his free hand vaguely. With any luck, he wouldn't be around to untangle the muddle of cars at the end of the day.

SIX

The developing confusion was, Abe decided, quite interesting. Given the freedom to park where they liked, most accelerated aggressively to the opposite end of the field and then, perhaps losing their nerve, bumpily reversed to the expanding tangled knot of cars, finally leaving their vehicle in such a way that they blocked at least one other person. There were exceptions to this, of course. They tended to be military looking individuals, their white moustaches bristling with disapproval as they searched hopelessly for a straight line to which they could attach themselves. They were equally disapproving of Abe when they and their straight-backed, pursed-mouthed wives marched past him to the school.

'You can see he's completely foreign,' said one curtly.

Mostly, however, the parents seemed content with his benign 'do as you like' approach. Abe, himself, didn't mind one way or the other; he was engaged with the far more pressing problem of how he was to get his team out of the school and on to the coach, which hadn't yet arrived, without anyone seeing them or stopping them. And there would be a driver to deal with too. Choices: kidnap driver? Fine in films but Abe had a suspicion that in real life it wouldn't be so easy. What coach driver would be frightened enough of the team and him and Alicia to do what they instructed?

'Take us to London.'

'Oh yes, looking for an old folks' home, are you?'

'Take us to London right now, or we'll do something terrible!'

'Got a frightening auntie somewhere, have you?'

No, only grown-ups, and probably with ugly scars, could do hi-jacking.

Bribery? A possibility, but he wasn't about to use any of his savings. So unless the vision had money to burn, bribery mightn't be the solution after all.

He glanced at his watch. An hour passed and then another. No one came to relieve him. The tangle of cars swelled across the field. It was coming up to midday. The last car had bumped into the field twenty minutes earlier, disgorging an exhausted looking mother in a pale floppy hat. 'I'm so terribly late,' she said as she hurried by Abe in a sort of half run, half walk, lumping along like a camel. How far away the desert seemed.

An enormous shape nudged up behind him and made a thunderous whooshing noise. Abe nearly jumped out of his skin.

The coach! He stepped back out of the way and then watched as it pulled around to the edge of the field. It was silver and sleek, its windows mysteriously black. It was wonderful. Perfect. An escape vehicle to die for. They could stuff the team in there and it wouldn't matter how they behaved.

'That's fine there,' called out Abe, intrigued to see what Mrs Dunne's special guests looked like. He gave what he imagined was a cheery thumbs up to the darkened front window and then waited.

The door hissed open, and an absurdly tall, thin woman, dressed in a long black trouser suit somehow unfolded herself down the steps. Another, differently shaped but similarly dressed followed the first, and another and another, all dark, as if the shadowy interior of the bus had compressed itself into human forms and was now spilling them out into the midday sun. They were all women, all smart, elegant even. There was something of the model in some of them, like Mrs Dunne herself, though they all seemed younger. Some walked in pairs, some on their own, all of them unhesitatingly, purposefully, straight towards the school.

'If you keep to the right of the main building you'll see the marquee . . . ' his voice trailed off.

'We know where to go,' said the tall, thin leader.

Her face, now he saw her close up, was powdery white, her lips a dark, purply red. She looked straight at him but with absolutely no interest whatever. He had the curious sensation of shrinking down to the size of a grub. And then she had passed by, and he blinked; the odd feeling was gone. A convention, he thought. Business. Then the blinding obviousness of what he was seeing struck him: witches. Like her, of course they were.

Abe was suddenly overcome with an urge to be very polite. 'A thousand welcomes,' he tried, bowing his head slightly like he thought a sheikh might. They ignored him. All of them, that is, apart from one. She was with a small group of ladies waiting at the foot of the bus's steps and she kept turning his way. Finally the woman they had been waiting for emerged from the coach. Wordlessly the group turned to go but the one who had shown some interest in Abe separated herself from the others and stalked towards him.

Abe bowed with renewed urgency. I do not want to be here, he chanted silently to himself. I want to be in the marquee, or my bed, or . . .

'Nasfali, what are you doing standing around wearing that ridiculous white coat? And will you please stop bobbing your head up and down like that.'

That voice! Abe felt as if he had been sloshed with icy water. He gasped and with some difficulty lifted his head. 'Hello, mother,' he said.

The group of women paused and turned towards them.

He felt nervous. He hated it when she looked at him like this. It made no difference that she was pale and beautiful; that her eyes were almond shaped, and her hair glossy black. He felt dissected. Why was she here? Not to see him run, that was for sure. Yet, here she was, one of Mrs Dunne's guests. Did that mean she was one of them?

Abe's mother sniffed. 'The coat, Nasfali, why are you

wearing the coat? I don't expect there is a good reason, but tell me anyway. It's too much to hope that you're about to do something useful.'

'I'm on duty.' She was so close he could smell the heavy, musky perfume she always wore, and yet she sounded as detached as if she were on the far side of the moon.

'Are you in trouble?'

'No.' It was an automatic response.

'Well,' she said. Obviously some vague idea of duty completed, Abe's mother walked swiftly over to join the group now waiting for her.

'I didn't know you had a boy,' he heard one of them say to his mother.

'Odd,' said another.

'And inconvenient,' added a third. There was a shiver of laughter and then they passed like a shadow across the drive and disappeared from view.

Abe expelled the breath he hadn't been aware of holding and shuddered. Then he peeled off his white coat and wiped his face. Having his mother unexpectedly arrive like this was just more trouble, piling up like a storm cloud or freak wave, ready to crash down on all of them. He sighed. What would Alicia say? At least she would be pleased about the bus. This thought prompted him to go and talk to the driver.

The door was still open, so Abe put his foot on the first step and poked his head in.

'Off!'

And he would have done too, but the driver's appearance surprised him. Coach drivers, Abe knew, were grumpy middle-aged men, in blue jackets, white shirts, and stripy ties. This one was a girl, not much older than Alicia, her eyes hidden behind jet-black glasses, a thick book open on her lap.

'I thought you might like a cup of tea or something,' said Abe, his mind beginning to pick up speed again, wondering if she were perhaps a student, earning extra money, needing funds, and so perhaps willing to switch cargoes, as it were, for a little bribe. 'I have a proposition,' he said.

'Don't be stupid.' She leaned forward slightly and the doors hissed shut but so swiftly that Abe had to snatch his foot out of the way.

'So you don't want the tea,' he said to the darkened glass. 'How about strawberries? I can do you a deal on strawberries.' Abe turned away and slung his coat over his shoulder. She would have to leave the coach at some stage in the afternoon. It would be easy. He and Alicia could take turns to watch and then they could nip on as soon as her back was turned. Foolish rude girl: she would have no bribe, no coach, but some very cross customers.

Time to meet up with the others. He hurried past the front of the school to the main playing field. Off to the left a cricket match was in progress. He could hear the occasional clop as bat hit cricket ball followed by the lonely calling of one parent: 'Well done, Johnny!' Most people, however, were making their way to the marquee. He hoped Alicia was keeping a keen eye on the team. Despite her assurances, he wasn't at all confident that Griffin and company were capable of behaving properly. Parents didn't flick towels, shove each other around, and giggle.

He saw Mrs Dunne emerging from the tent, her nose tilted up as if scenting trouble. Then she greeted a mother and father escorting their son to the marquee, and ushered them inside.

He joined the thickening tide of families and within moments found himself wedged between a woman in a flowery dress on one side and a determined family on the other. 'Is it going to be stwawbewwies and cweam for us?' demanded the little determined girl of the group.

'If we hurry,' said the determined father, giving a determined shove forward.

The woman in the flowery dress gave Abe a cross look. 'Don't push, young man.'

'I'm sorry,' muttered Abe, 'I, um . . .' but the woman was already forging her way through the entrance.

Someone else jabbed Abe in the ribs. These parents were worse than the First Years. 'Do you mind!' he said turning to confront a small, fat man in a cream sports jacket which didn't quite fit.

'Gotcha,' said the man and bumped him with his very round stomach. Abe was knocked sideways into the determined father who simply shoved him back again.

Abe scowled at the fat man, who grinned at him. 'It's me,' hissed the fat man, 'cracking rig, don't you think.' The man had a blue silk scarf round his neck, tied up like a cravat. It strongly reminded Abe of a scarf that Mrs Dunne wore sometimes . . .

'Roberts!'

'Spot on, Sherlock. Never have guessed, would you?'

Abe grabbed Roberts by the arm, guided him through the opening, and then had to haul him off to one side to stop him making a beeline for the food. 'Where is everyone?'

'What's the panic?' said Roberts peering anxiously over his shoulder at the diminishing piles of sandwiches. 'Most of them will be in here by now. The girl told us not to go round in a mob so we split up. It's good fun, isn't it?'

Abe scanned the interior of the marquee: most of the space was given over to the platform and ranks of empty chairs; the area by the entrance was where the food was. There was Alicia all right, dishing out strawberries. Then, scattered through the crowd, he picked out the various members of the team. The headmaster was up on the rostrum, tapping a microphone, getting ready for the speeches. He could even see the dark-suited women from the coach scattered about. They didn't appear to be mingling, or concentrating on food, but simply watching. One or two of them, he noticed, had little notebooks into which they occasionally jotted something. And there was Mrs Dunne coming up beside her husband and saying something into his bushy ear.

The microphone barked and whistled and everyone clearly heard 'Good Lord!' erupt tinnily from the speakers. Then there was a click as Mrs Dunne reached past her husband and switched the microphone off.

Abe cut through the crowd to Alicia.

'Have to talk to you,' he said.

'No,' she said, 'I have to talk to you.' She served another parent and then without turning her head said, 'Be very careful, she's watching.'

Abe scooped a spoonful of strawberries into his mouth, deliberately keeping his head lowered and his back half-turned to Alicia. 'What does she know?'

'What? Don't speak with your mouth full.'

Abe swallowed. 'What's she know?'

'She has the photograph. Didn't have time to hide it properly, so she knows the team's out.'

'Freaking . . .'

'Pharaohs, yes.'

'But they're all in here. What'll we do?'

'Get them out.'

A squawk from the microphone interrupted them. 'Just a quick notice, ladies and gentlemen, before the proceedings get under way. A reminder that all students spending Saturday night away with their parents must sign the sign-out register in the main hall and Mrs Dunne will, of course, be there to check that you're looking all ship-shape and what-not. The remaining rascals will have high tea in the big hall and that's where their registration will take place. Now, if everyone would like to move away from the grub and down to the seats here, we can dish out a few of these prizes.'

The movement away from the food was a little less urgent than the earlier surge towards it had been but eventually Abe and Alicia found themselves on the margins of the crowd. And with Mrs Dunne now out of sight, and the headmaster settling into his comfortable drone, a drone punctuated by polite applause for the prize winners, they could talk more easily. 'I should be getting one of those,' said Abe.

'Concentrate, Nasfali. That rubbish about registration, they never do that normally, do they?'

'No.'

'Exactly. She hopes to check every boy in the school and so find the team.'

'That's because she knows——'

'No, she doesn't know, that's exactly the point,' said Alicia, with the beginnings of impatience. 'She doesn't know, Nasfali, that they're not boys. She doesn't know that they've turned into dumpy old men. She doesn't know half as much as she thinks she does. We can get them out any time we want. Have you got the coach sorted?'

'Not exactly,' said Abe. He drew her through the flap at the rear of the marquee. A few drops of rain started to fall, plopping fatly on the canvas behind them. The playing field was deserted; the entire small school somehow squeezed into the tent. He told her of his encounter with his mother and the strangely suited women and of his plan to spy on the coach driver.

'Knew you were different, Nasfali.'

'Of course,' said Abe, a little puzzled and taken aback by this, 'I am half Egyptian, if that's what you mean.'

'Not that——your mum; she's one of them.' She gripped his arm. 'Face it, Nasfali, you're like me; your mother's a witch.'

'But she doesn't do anything,' protested Abe. 'She doesn't . . . broomstick,' he ended helplessly.

'She doesn't have to. Believe me. Now tell me about the driver. Young,' said Alicia, 'like me? Reading a book? What book? Did you see the title?' She seemed consumed by an interest that Abe couldn't understand. No, he hadn't seen what she was reading, and the funny thing was that when he tried to visualize it, there was no title. 'Apprentice,' she sniffed, 'here to learn. Well, she'll learn something all right.'

'What?'

'That,' said Alicia, 'they can't always do what they want.'

'And we can?'

'We can try. What do you say, Nasfali? You don't want to back out now, do you?'

'No.'

'You know what this means,' she said, fixing Abe with her earnest, black-eye-shadowed eyes, 'no going back, for both of us. That'll be it.'

'I don't want to come back here,' said Abe. 'I'm going to Cairo.'

'Are you?' Something that might pass for a smile crossed Alicia's face. 'You might be safe there, who knows. Who knows, I might even come out with you. I can't do anything here.'

Abe couldn't tell whether she was being serious or not, so he assumed a solemn expression and told her that his family there would make her most welcome. He didn't mention the fact that this family only existed in his imagination. However, she seemed impressed, which was good. Then, together, they worked out how to organize the team. They would take it in turns to watch the coach; Alicia would take the last watch at six that afternoon. The driver, they reckoned, would have to go and get some tea or something by then.

Abe slipped back into the tent, found Griffin, who quickly grasped the situation and promised to set up a rota to watch the coach and report to Alicia or Abe as soon as the driver left it empty.

Griffin was first, then Thomas, then Jack, and the hours slipped by. Parents left, students were registered. Mrs Dunne smiled and talked graciously, but her eyes scoured every child who came before her.

To Abe the team, even though they were being good about sticking to twos and threes rather than clustering together in one gang, seemed to stick out like so many sore thumbs and as more and more families left so they became more obvious. Eventually Abe spotted Captain Dunne going up to Gannet. He hurried over to try to head him off but was too late. Instead he caught snatches of their conversation.

'Yes. Yes, Lloyd's,' Gannet drawled. 'Lloyd's. Merchant bank. Scoops of dosh. Tidy investment and Coutts, of course. There you have it, cracking really.'

'Splendid,' murmured the headmaster, 'very good show indeed,' and he steamed off, clearly satisfied that this beaky nosed over-aged thirteen year old was something big in the City and would be willing to invest huge sums of money in his school. What the headmaster didn't hear was the loud raspberry Gannet blew as soon as he was out of range. 'He's bonkers as a bishop, isn't he?' he said to Abe, grinning at his own performance.

'Yes, but she,' answered Abe nodding towards Mrs Dunne, 'is not.' Discreetly he herded the team out of the tent, round to the back of the school, then sneaked them up to his dormitory and told them to wait. No one would disturb them; all the other boys had gone home already.

Abe then mooched down to the library to meet Alicia who reported bad news: the driver had not left the coach. She clearly had a constitution of iron; no need for food or a bathroom. The team, they decided, would have to stay in Abe's room all night if they had to. Alicia would keep watch on the coach and call them at the first chance. If the worst came to the worst, she would get them up at five and they would just walk to the railway station.

SEVEN

'**H**urry! Get up!'

Abe woke and saw Alicia, face pale as a barn owl, peering down at him.

'What time is it?'

'Ten.'

'Shouldn't we wake the others?' he said. Conscious that he had gone to bed in his underpants, he was scrabbling for his trousers and then clumsily pulling them on under the bedclothes.

'Is that always how you dress in a hurry?'

'Always.' He swung his legs out of the bed. 'The others?'

'No, we'll get them later. There's something you have to see.'

Before he had finished buttoning his shirt, she grabbed his hand and tugged him towards the door. 'What is it?'

But she wouldn't answer. They hurried along silent corridors, up a flight to another passage where it was so dark they had to feel their way along the wall, and then through a doorway. Then Alicia stopped. 'We're right over mother's office. Put your ear to the floor.'

Fully awake now but disorientated and tense because of the hushed and hurried way she was whispering, he did as he was told. He could hear the faint murmur of voices. 'Her guests?'

'Yes. Be very quiet.'

She moved away. There was a whispering sound that startled him. 'Oh,' he gasped, the hairs on the back of his neck prickling as the room suddenly flooded with moonlight.

'What is it?' she hissed, her hand on the curtain she'd just drawn back.

'I thought that was magic,' he whispered. 'Very sorry.'
'Don't be silly.'

They were in a little room with a makeshift table with a computer monitor on it. Alicia tiptoed over to the table and touched a switch on the side of the monitor. After a blip and flickers of green, a picture began to take shape, pin-sized to begin with but, as it expanded, very sharp.

There, on the screen, Abe saw Mrs Dunne at one end of the room and, in a semicircle a couple of rows deep, there were her 'guests', his mother included.

'You can spy on them!'

'It's called surveillance, Nasfali. Technology. I don't need magic,' she said coolly.

They could see everything. Abe could even spot the coach driver, devoid of sunglasses, but looking even more like a student in uniform, sitting in the back row, an open pad on her lap on to which she was making careful notes.

Alicia pressed another switch and Mrs Dunne's voice whispered into the room.

' . . . And that is why my family run Prackton Hall.' Mrs Dunne paused, eyeing her guests. They knew perfectly well what the school's purpose was, but in her view it did no harm to remind them. 'The boys don't know, of course; nor their parents; not even my dear, loyal, and stupid husband. But you do, because we're sisters.'

'Sisters,' murmured her dark-suited audience. They were listening carefully, even the one on the far right with her long legs stretched out and crossed at the ankle, studying her nails. They were listening because Delia Dunne was a powerful and influential witch as had been her mother, and her mother's mother before her. It was her family, females only, of course, who had guided the sisterhood out of the dark ages of persecution, when any ugly old crone, or, for that matter, dark-haired beauty could be dragged off to the ducking chair, or to the stake to be cooked to a crisp.

'The boys here are well trained,' continued Mrs Dunne, 'and will make ideal husbands for your daughters. Ideal because they will never question you, never see you for what you are, and, most usefully, once they've served their purpose can be discarded.' The audience nodded and smiled. 'Your daughters,' Abe's mother shifted in her chair, 'will have daughters and we will grow in number and strength, and respectability. We already have a sister in the cabinet, how long before one of us becomes first minister?'

'Not long at all,' chorused the sisters.

'Nobody talks about witches any more: too childish, fairy tales, nonsense, superstition, but we breed and feed and multiply. Nobody knows us for what we are, because we are smart, elegant . . . and looking about me not only beautiful but very, very rich.

'Things are good,' said Mrs Dunne and then paused. 'However I am worried. As most of you know, thirteen years ago, one of us, my own blood sister, had a son.' There was a ripple of unease; the few who had witnessed Abe's words with his mother at the car park, looked at her with raised eyebrows. 'That is the first time this has happened in centuries.'

The sisters leaned forward and joined in. Was the boy a problem? Could he not be . . . 'solved' or, as one of them suggested with a brittle laugh, 'dissolved'? How could a single boy upset the way things were? 'Give him to us,' they murmured. Abe's mother studied her nails. 'Give him to us.'

'Sisters.' Mrs Dunne held up a hand to quieten them. 'He's not really the problem, merely a small irritation. He resists me, but he doesn't know that he is resisting me.' She smiled, a little indulgently. 'He will change and become like the others. Or I'll crush him. That is, of course, if you don't mind, my dear,' she said addressing her sister.

Abe's mother shrugged. 'Why should I mind?' she replied.

'Exactly,' agreed Mrs Dunne. 'The boy himself is nothing. My real worry is that he is part of a pattern. For instance, have any of you, my dears, had problems, things not going as smoothly as they should, old spells, perhaps, becoming unwound in a rather disagreeable fashion?' She eyed the gathering and nodded. There were pursed lips, tightened shoulders, cuffs straightened. 'No sister likes to admit her power might be slipping, does she, but I can see you too have your worries. Maybe only little things, but you have noticed, haven't you?'

They had.

'Well, you're not alone,' continued Mrs Dunne and then, a little more briskly, she revealed her own experience with the boys of 1942, glossing over some of the details, particularly her crush on young Bink Roberts. 'I have to get them back, of course,' she explained, 'otherwise it might get into the papers and you know how television is such a curse. Do we really want awful ordinary people believing in us again . . . and hearing of our "activities"?'

No, they certainly did not.

'No. Exactly. They can't have made their escape from here yet. And eleven boys in football shorts at the end of the summer term shouldn't be too hard to find—' an ugly scowl crossed her face, 'but I have scoured the place for them—'

'Had you not thought,' cut in Abe's mother, 'that the boys you dealt with are now probably as old as you, or even a bit older.'

Mrs Dunne had not thought of this. The lobes of Mrs Dunne's ears burned crimson. She smiled at her sister. 'Of course,' she said. 'But I think the problem is a little more complex than you possibly realize because, you see, it involves my daughter.'

There were gasps of astonishment at this.

'How?'

'Not possible!'

'She refuses to be what she is; she refuses to be one of us. What's more I'm quite certain that she's involved with the disappearance of the 1942 boys from the photograph I put them in.'

The effect of this statement was as if you had squealed broken glass across a blackboard. She folded her hands neatly in front of her and waited for the uproar to die down. 'In the old days,' shouted one of the guests, who looked far too young and stylish to be shouting any such thing, 'we would have had her turned into a rat . . . '

'Or worse, perhaps,' agreed Mrs Dunne smoothly, 'but, my dears, think: the old days were not so good at all. Can we afford to lose our self discipline? Do we want people to know about our spells and magic? No, we don't. Not now. Later perhaps, when it is too late for them to even try to persecute us. We must be discreet. We must do what we have to do but without anyone knowing; we must be sly; we must be cunning. With your help a restraining spell will do until we can tackle this business of the team from 1942.'

The suggestion that she be turned into a rat had Alicia fuming; the threat of a restraining spell had blown away her cool completely.

'Did you hear them? Did you hear her! She's seriously out of order. A rat! What a witch!'

'And she's my aunt!' Abe shuddered.

'Your aunt? She's my mother!'

'Yes. Goodness!' He slapped his forehead. 'Do you realize you're my cousin?'

'I'll be your rat cousin if we don't get out of here now!'

'How do you turn this off?'

'Forget that. Go. Go. Go.'

As if there was a fireball at their backs, the pair were steering their way through the dark upper floors of the school; they were rattling down a spiral stone staircase; they were banging through the dormitory door.

'Up!' shouted Abe. Being quiet didn't matter now. Their only hope was to be out of the building and in that coach before the meeting broke up.

'Come on! Come on!' He shook Griffin, he yanked Stokely's foot, he slapped Thomas's thigh. 'Up or she'll find you; she'll turn you into rats' gizzards!' He prodded Jissop. 'She'll make you eat dust for ever!' And he stripped the bedding from Gannet.

As they stumbled to their feet, groaning, Alicia poked their arms into their jackets and shirts, found them their shoes and jostled and hustled until scraggy, dishevelled, white hair bristling up like hedgehogs, trousers in some cases on the wrong bodies, they were assembled at the door.

'What happens with a restraining spell?' asked Abe just before they reopened the dormitory door.

She shook her head. 'Could be anything. Don't even know if she needs me there for the spell.'

'Lead the way,' said Abe. 'If you fall or something we'll just pick you up and drag you along.'

'Very nice,' sniffed Alicia, but she led the way all the same.

Gambling that her mother and the witches were still penned up in her business room, she took a direct route to the front door, past matron's—Miss Chirt was asleep with her head on the table, a half empty green bottle within easy reach—down to the corridor where Abe had hung on the radiator and then along to the main hall. The whole school seemed asleep. And the team were finding it difficult to wake up properly: they yawned and bumped into each other.

'Mother's put the place to sleep,' explained Alicia, 'so she won't be disturbed.'

'Then why not us?' Abe was wide awake and so was she.

'Dunno,' said Alicia. 'Maybe she can't.' She pulled open the front door, grabbed the first member of the team to hand and shoved him through. 'Straight to the car park and wait.' Off stumbled Bittern and then Pike and then Jonson and Thomas, into the darkness. Within seconds half the team were through the door and then Alicia went, easily outstripping those in front of her.

Abe took over. He ushered out Jack, Gannet, and Griffin, a moment's pause and then the last batch. As he quietly pulled the door behind him, he heard a sudden surge of voices from upstairs. They were on the move!

He hurried the old boys across the open drive, until finally they were all in the field, screened from the school by trees and hedge. And there gleaming dully in the moonlight was the coach.

The activity, the cool night air, and maybe being outside the bounds of whatever slight sleeping spell Mrs Dunne had cast on the school, had brought the team fully awake.

'What now, skipper?' said Griffin.

Abe was bothered. He couldn't see Alicia in the group. Had she been 'got'? 'Try the door,' he said. Should they go without her?

'It's locked.'

They weren't going anywhere.

'Wait here,' said Abe. 'We'll have this sorted in no time.'

'No time. Half time. Good time. Past time,' chanted Jack and Jissop.

'In a jiffy,' snickered Griffin.

'And jig time.' Roberts performed a portly jig.

'Roberts, you're a prune. A Celtic prune at that.'

'Off you go, skipper.'

Abe turned and ran back across the field and bumped straight into Alicia hurrying away from the garage. 'I was just wrecking mother's car,' she said, 'or rather, putting a restraining spell on it.'

'What?'

'It's a joke,' she said. 'My mother doesn't make jokes; but I can.'

Abe didn't like to say that it wasn't a very good joke so instead he said: 'You are magnificent, Alicia.'

Striding swiftly ahead of him, Alicia didn't appear to hear the compliment. When she reached the locked coach, she pushed her way through the team, gave the door a sharp rap with her knuckle, pulled down the handle, and the door murmured open. 'Watched the driver locking it like this,' she said to the impressed onlookers. 'On you all get.'

There was a scrummage, the team pushing to pile in the back, leaving Alicia and Abe, like a couple of sad teachers, sitting in the front.

The door closed.

The bus, not surprisingly since there was no driver sitting in her seat, remained stationary.

EIGHT

'No driver,' said Abe. 'Did you think of that?'

'Did you?'

Abe shook his head. 'No.'

Alicia twizzled her nose ring. 'Me neither.' And she made a noise that Abe thought might be a laugh.

He didn't think it was funny. Through the trees, he could see lights coming on in the main building, one room after another. The search had started. In the back of the bus, a kind of calm had settled after the seat scrummage, a calm that lasted for all of five seconds before a raspy voice broke into: 'Why are we waiting?' Another joined in and then they were all at it.

He stood up. 'Can anyone drive?' he shouted over their singing.

Instantly the singing stopped and they all shouted, 'Me!' 'I can!' and started to surge out of their seats.

'No,' said Abe. 'Go back.' He was face to face with Thomas.

'Really,' he said. 'I am brilliant at driving my dad's tractor. This old bus would be a cinch.' Abe was about to explain that this old bus probably bore as much relation to his dad's tractor as a space ship to a coracle, when the engine roared into life and the bus gave a great jerk backwards, which sent Thomas and the three or four squashed up behind him lurching into Abe.

Abe fought his way out from the elbows and knees, as the bus rampaged wildly round the empty car parking field, thumping over bumps which flung its back end off the ground like a bucking wild pony. He gripped two seats for support and turned. Alicia was in the driver's seat! It was just as well that he did have a good hold, because the bus suddenly braked and then rammed forward which sent Thomas and pals spinning back to their seats.

Abe worked his way forward to where Alicia sat hunched over the big wheel, her face tight with concentration. 'Where's that gate?' she said.

'There!' said Abe, pointing off to the left, 'where the lights are. Why not turn on your own?'

She did and at the same time hauled the wheel round, so that at a bumpy twenty miles an hour and accelerating, they bore down on the gate, their headlights suddenly catching the crowd of women who were waving torches, as if signalling them to stop.

'It's your mother.'

'Yes. And yours.'

'What are they doing?'

'Trying to stop us, of course.'

As if on cue, the women, their faces stark white in the harsh glare of the headlights, raised their left arms and pointed at the bus.

Alicia gave a sudden 'hoof!' as if she had been whacked in the chest. She slumped back into her seat, her hands slipping from the wheel, her feet from the pedal. The bus lurched and Abe, crouching beside her, grabbed the wheel. There were piercing shrieks from outside and cheers from the back of the bus. And then suddenly they were through the gate, the women scattering and diving out of the way, unable to stop the careening bus which clipped one of the gateposts.

'Brakes!' shouted Abe as he saw that they were about to hit the drive at right angles; unless they could brake and turn they would smack straight into the trees on the far side.

He could hear the sound of Alicia sucking air into her lungs and then the bus gave a roar as she stamped on to the accelerator and yanked the wheel hard round to the left.

The bus skidded on the grass, then hit the drive with

a squeal, keeling right over on to two wheels and threatening to tip them upside down. But after a thunderous bump, Abe realized they were lashing down the drive with the speedo knocking on fifty.

'Whoo!' exclaimed Alicia, probing at the brake. 'That was fun.'

She slowed the bus at the main gate, and then confidently swept them out into the thin night-time traffic.

Abe looked back. 'No sign of them following,' he said.

'They can't,' she said. 'I told you I fixed mother's car.'

'Impressive,' said Abe. 'I didn't know you could drive.'

'Nothing to it.' She glanced up at Abe, her rings glinting in the dashboard light. 'Relax, Nasfali. You can leave this bit to me.'

'OK.' Abe went down the bus and quietened the team, who were still crashing about after the excitement of the escape, then he took his seat behind Alicia.

Truly a vision, he thought, and he imagined her wearing the same garb of pink dress, heavy boots, and purple eye shadow, driving a coach out to Giza and there would be ladies wearing chador, veiled and black-clothed, tourists in panama hats, and bare-legged boys in rubber sandals and old men watching from open doorways, and in and through the hotch-potch tangle of colour and people, Alicia Dunne would cruise her silver coach right to the towering steps of the Great Pyramid itself.

All of a sudden Abe remembered the particular day, two weeks after his sixth birthday, when he found a thick blue letter with an Egyptian stamp on it. There was, he remembered, a pyramid on the stamp and he had asked his mother who had sent it to her. 'A mistake,' she had said. The person who had sent it to her had been a mistake, and when he had gone on and on asking who the person was, she had told him that it had been his father and she had held up her forefinger, the one with the silver ring with squiggles on it, and had told him his father had been weak and stupid and she didn't ever want to be reminded of him again.

'But you said he was dead.'

'He is.'

'How can he be if he—'

'He is.' And she had torn up the letter without even opening it and thrown the tiny pieces in the bin. 'If you turn out to be at all like him,' she had said, 'I'll put you in a sack and the rubbish men will take you away.'

That night he had crept out of his room and retrieved as many of the little scraps of blue paper as he could find and he had tried, tried so hard to put all of them back into order; but all he had ever managed were little islands of information: names of streets, of people, and then bits of promises: 'I will bring you such things . . . ', 'you will be queen . . . ', 'you will live for . . . '

It was then he first dreamed of going to Cairo.

His mother found the torn letter and while he watched round-eyed she placed the scraps on a plate, set light to them with a candle. He watched the blue paper flare suddenly and then dissolve into white ash. Then, briskly, she broke eggs into a pan, whipping them into an omelette. 'Your supper. Watch.' And she blew the ash into the pan and folded the omelette over it. 'Eat.'

He wouldn't; she did. Now that he thought about it, it was the first witch-like thing he had seen her do.

The bus was quiet, humming along, Alicia humming along with it. 'Did you ever get on all right with your mother and father?' asked Abe.

'Is that question serious, Nasfali? Sometimes you disappoint me.'

Being a disappointment to the vision was not what Abe intended. 'I was just thinking about mine, you know.'

'No.'

'I was a mistake.'

75

'Anyone could see that.'

'No, I should have been a girl.'

Alicia snorted. 'I wouldn't let the team hear you talk like that, they'll make your life a misery.'

'Magic,' said Abe. 'It's mother to daughter, that's what they said. That's why my mum doesn't have anything to do with me. If I'd been a girl though, I could have been a witch. It would have made getting to Egypt a bit easier maybe.'

'Would you want to be a girl, then?' Alicia glanced over her shoulder and the bus made a sudden swoop up on to the pavement. 'Whoops.'

'Not now, course I wouldn't, because I'm a boy, aren't I, but if I'd been born different, then it wouldn't have bothered the different me, would it?'

'You'd have made quite a nice girl.'

Abe wasn't sure if that was a compliment. 'Aren't you interested in magic and stuff, Alicia? Your mother's really powerful. Perhaps you could be too, but good . . . '

'Flashing eyes and flames from my fingertips?'

'Yes,' said Abe, very taken by the image, 'you would be magnificent.'

'Boring,' said Alicia. 'Rules, learning lists as long as your arm, ending up marrying someone like my dad. Who wants that? Witches don't laugh, Nasfali. And that's a fact. I intend to lead my own life, thank you very much, and that does not include wearing deep-frozen grey suits. My mother can keep her magic. I,' she said firmly, 'am going to have fun.'

Alicia was now neatly nudging the bus into an unpromising looking alley.

'We can't stop here,' said Abe. 'Where are we going anyway?'

'To take the boys clubbing,' said Alicia. 'Do you want to have a party, boys?' she shouted to the back of the coach. 'Do you want to go to a nightclub?'

This elicited a round of sleepy cheers, a few slaps, and a rolled up pair of socks that sailed out from the back row of seats.

'You're joking,' said Abe. 'They won't let them in. Your mother will catch us. I mean, we just can't.'

The brakes gave a satisfying hiss. 'That's where you're wrong, Nasfali. I can do exactly what I want now. And this is the last place my mother would ever think of looking for me or them. As for getting in; they can hardly claim they're under age, can they.'

Abe reluctantly followed her down the steps. 'No, but . . . ' What he didn't want to admit to being worried about was that he had never been to a club; that he was way under age; and he didn't want to be stuck outside on his own.

Alicia took his arm. 'Lighten up, Nasfali. I'll get you in.'

There was broken glass underfoot, fly posters splattered on the walls, and a small group of lads just making their way past the bouncers and through a nondescript doorway. 'Everyone follow me,' said Alicia, once the team were off the bus, 'and don't open your mouths until we're in.' Abe cuffed Jack who had immediately opened his mouth as wide as he could.

'What's this lot?' said the bouncer, barely glancing at Alicia's ID, and nodding towards the team. From somewhere below their feet they could feel and hear the heavy thud thud of the music.

'From the council,' said Alicia briskly. 'Research and sanitation.'

'Fair enough,' said the bouncer, and his partner, both of them as bulky as letter boxes in their black bomber jackets, wedged open the door and stood back to let them go past.

Abe waited for the team to go by as, slowly, Alicia

checked them in one by one at the little glass–fronted pay desk. The lobby was tiny and the team were squeezing in together like fat sardines.

'Not you, sunshine.' A large hand planted itself on Abe's chest.

'I'm with them.'

'Not tonight, Irene. On your banana boat.'

He took his foot away and the door would have closed, except Roberts's large backside was in the way. Fortunately, Alicia, who had been looking around to check whether they were all in, suddenly saw half of Abe beginning to back away. She shoved through to the door and grabbed Abe's arm. 'He's with me,' she said, very clearly, her eyes fixed on the bouncer.

'Oh,' said the bouncer, looking momentarily troubled, 'right then. In you go, squire.'

Alicia tugged Abe through the door while the other bouncer was asking: 'Why d'yer let him in, then?'

'He was with her, wasn't he?'

The door closed and they were safe.

'Down the stairs,' said Alicia raising her voice over the thickening sound of the music, and making pointing motions with her arm. The team, however, seemed a bit reluctant to lead the way. They nudged and prodded and tried to get Stokely to go first but he wouldn't. Alicia's mouth twitched in a near smile. 'We'll lead the way, then.'

The stairs were steep, the light dim, the music rumbled and thundered louder and louder with each step they took, and the air began to steam. 'Here we go,' shouted Alicia and they stepped into the space.

The music was a wall of sound that banged their lungs and streamed sweatily down the walls. Spiky haired dancers in low slung baggy jeans and ripped T-shirts bounced and waved their arms, cheerfully slopping beer from glasses on to the floor and themselves as they weaved and leapt like frenzied robots. Lights erupted in time to the bass and in the far corner a DJ presided over his decks and mixer, nodding his head happily like a TV puppet.

One after the other the team nudged into the room, mouths open, fingers in ears for some, eyes staring half terrified, half mesmerized. Alicia caught Griffin's eye. 'Go and dance,' she mouthed.

A dancer swooped by. 'It's the wrinklies,' he yelled cheerfully. 'Far out!'

Griffin cocked his head on one side. Then grinding his arms like a steam locomotive, he suddenly puffed his way out on to the floor. And the others exploded with laughter and immediately copied him.

Alicia led Abe along the edge of the floor till they came to a free alcove where she ducked in behind a table. Abe slid in beside her. 'Well,' she said, putting her head close to his so that he could hear without her having to shout, 'what next?'

While the team steam-engined to the music, Abe and Alicia tried to figure out the next stage. Abe wanted somehow to leak the story to the newspapers, make the team so well known that they could hold a sponsored football match for senior citizens that would raise enough money to take them all off to Cairo and somehow there would be his family and maybe there would even be a granny to look after the team, 'and then we'll have one big match in front of the Great Pyramid.'

'And then what?'

Abe hadn't thought that far.

'I think,' said Alicia, 'that the simplest thing is if we take them home. I know,' she said, seeing Abe about to object, 'that some of their homes will have gone, but not all. Think. Long-lost children? Rewards? Yes? And then you can go to Cairo.'

'All right,' agreed Abe. 'I suppose you're right, but just imagine a match in front of the pyramid. At night. You know. Full moon. Make a fortune, wouldn't it?'

There was a sudden roar from the dance floor as the first thundering guitar chords scoured out of the sound system.

Bodies rafted together into a big mosh in the centre of the room; the team, excited but clearly fading fast, jogged blithely out of time to the beat on the edge of the floor. The song moved to its sinister refrain: 'And you do as they told you', but before its final explosion, something seemed to happen. The refrain stuck, the beat stuck, the lights throbbed. 'And you do as they told you . . . And you do as they told you . . . And you do as they told you . . . ' and the dancers stuck too, jerking and bouncing mechanically, uniformly, unchangingly.

'Look.' Alicia pointed as four black-bomber-jacketed bouncers bulged out from the stairway, their heads slowly scanning the crowd.

'I'm not imagining this, am I,' said Abe, 'but don't they all look like Lakin?' Four heads, faces, fat and greasy like the school chef's, all identical.

'No,' said Alicia, 'not unless I'm imagining it too. Mother must be close.' She pointed to the team, standing in a line, jigging slower and slower like wind-up toys running down. 'Let's get them out. See the exit there. First one. Go!'

The nearest member of the team was Stokely. Abe shook him hard, till he blinked and focused. Abe pointed out the exit. 'Lead the way,' he mouthed. As Stokely moved off, Abe took Jack's hand, who was next in line, and fastened it on to Stokely's shirt tail. And so, very quickly, between the two of them, they made the team into a monkey tail trail, and then ushered them as quickly as they could behind the thick wall of hypnotized dancers towards the exit, while the bouncers moved like sharks nosing for the kill, shoving bodies out of the way, gathering speed.

'Oi! Jam-boy!'

Abe pushed Gannet through the door and turned to

see one of the bouncers only a couple of steps away from them. 'Quick!' He tried to make Alicia go ahead of him but she shook him off.

'You first!' she shouted, turning to face the thick-bodied bouncer while Abe stumbled into the street.

He glimpsed her pointing and heard her snap: 'Get back, you worm!' The next second she was beside him while the Lakin bouncer seemed to freeze, just for an instant, and then lurched after her. Abe grabbed the door and slammed it as hard as he could.

There was a fat roar but the door failed to close. Four stubby red fingers were curled round the edge. 'Push!' said Alicia. 'Hard as you can, Nasfali.' Abe banged his shoulder against the door and there was another roar of pain and then the door juddered as the other bouncers threw their weight at the door from the inside.

'We can't hold them,' gasped Abe. Inch by inch the gap was widening. The boom of the bass, and the growling refrain: 'You do as they told you . . . ' thundered out into the alley. 'Run for it. Now!'

They both released the door at the same moment and sprinted for the coach. Behind them, the Lakins tumbled off balance on to the pavement, but the team were all safely on board and Alicia and Abe had a precious couple of yards lead and were able to swing themselves up and close the door before the first Lakin hurled himself howling at the side of the coach, thundering his fists against the side.

There was no scrummaging around this time, no whoops or yells from the team. For this, their second escape in one night, they were exhausted and frightened. Alicia gunned the engine and the coach squealed forward, leaving their pursuers scrabbling along on the outside and then rapidly falling behind. Alicia glanced into the side mirror. 'Mother's little helpers,' she said. 'I think we'll leave them behind, don't you.'

'Yes,' said Abe, 'if you don't mind.'

Part Two

Inside the City

NINE

'I thought you said we'd be safe,' said Abe to the top of Alicia's head, which is all he could see from where he was sitting behind the driver's seat. She didn't hear or didn't choose to hear, so Abe, knowing he was being a bit self-righteous but somehow unable to stop himself, began to repeat what he had said: 'I thought . . . '

'Safe!' Alicia sniffed.

'Well?'

'We'll go to London.'

'No. We'll find out which of the team lives . . . lived,' he corrected himself, 'closest.'

'OK,' she said, 'you do that, Nasfali.'

A police car, its blue light flickering, swept down the far side of the dual carriageway, heading back into the town while they, having jumped three lights in a row and broken the speed limit, cruised quietly north.

Abe went down the centre aisle and spoke to Griffin who was still wide awake, clicking the little pull down tray down and up, and humming away to himself. It seemed that Stokely's family were nearest; they had a farm in west Sussex, near a village called Ashington.

They took the next turning left and made their way cross country.

'How did they do that, find us so easily?' asked Abe. 'And those men, the bouncers, all like Lakin, weren't they. It just wasn't real.'

'Real? Of course it was real. She's a witch; she can make anything real. Haven't you worked that one out? What's more important, Nasfali,' she said swinging the bus round a roundabout and taking the Ashington exit, 'is that they didn't catch us. That's what counts. Now where?'

It was two thirty as they nosed slowly down a black winding lane, turned right at a tiny shadowy church, tucked in behind a high bank, and then left through a set of farm gates. 'It's over there,' said Stokely excitedly. As they drew closer, their headlights picked out a large building surrounded by outbuildings, high walls, and tall black gates. 'It's a bit changed,' he said, the excitement now tinged with doubt. 'We just lived in one end of that building; the other half was a barn.'

The bus stopped with a soft whoosh of the brakes. At the same moment intruder lights bathed them, the gates, and the vast courtyard, which they now saw was nestling with expensive cars, in a bright light. 'Oh,' said Stokely. 'Oh dear. It looks so different I don't know whether I do live here any more.'

Stokely was so confused by what he was seeing that Abe decided to get out and try the gates. He found a buzzer and a metallic voice curtly told him that no one in Dapple-down Retreat had heard of a family called Stokely, and they certainly didn't accept coach tours, if that was what they were, at any time of the day or night, and if they didn't go away instantly they would call the police.

'Thank you,' said Abe.

'You're welcome,' said the voice.

They backed up, turned and drove into the main village, stopping at a telephone box, to see if there were any Stokelys in the local directory; there weren't.

'I don't mind really, honestly I don't. I'm sure we'll find them soon.' Stokely turned away quickly and took a seat on his own midway down the coach. Griffin ducked his head out to stare at his unfortunate team mate and then nudged Bink Roberts and whispered something to him.

'Probably saw you coming, Stoker,' called out Jack, 'and hid round the back.'

Some of them laughed at this, few recognized that they themselves might soon be in the same small, grey haired situation. Stokely didn't laugh and Abe couldn't think of anything to say to comfort him. He'd been the first to say how much he wanted to go home. What chance was there of finding a family after sixty years, and a world war?

It was five o'clock in the morning when Abe woke up. They'd pulled into an all-night service station and Alicia was just coming on board. 'Do you rise and shine, Nasfali?' she said.

How extraordinary she was, he thought; nothing she said was ever quite what he expected. 'I rise,' he said.

They were in Vauxhall. Alicia had driven round London for most of the night, checking off the addresses that Abe had given her the night before; five of the team had lived in London. Bittern's house, perhaps destroyed in the Blitz, was now the site of a multi-storey car park, Gannet's a Tesco on the Cromwell Road. The garage forecourt they were currently parked on was what might have been the front garden to Roberts's house. Jonson's house was still there, on the Fulham Road, but had been converted into flats with no sign of the name Jonson on any of the bell plates. Only Jack's house appeared to be intact and was where it was supposed to be. Alicia proposed that they go back there after breakfast and let Jack try his luck, but she wasn't hopeful. 'Plan one, Nasfali, is a failure and so chances of us getting a reward are looking slim.' She checked her purse and made a face. 'Enough for breakfast, then I have to use mother's card.'

'You know her PIN number? I'm surprised she trusted you with it—not meaning to be offensive, of course.'

'Of course she doesn't trust me. What a horrible thought. If I were trusted by her I would have to be like her. Would you like to be like your mother?' Abe was tempted to say he was the wrong shape, but contented himself with a simple shake of the head.

'I'm glad to hear it. No one should be like her mother,'

she said and started the engine and rolled out on to the road.

'Or father?' asked Abe. 'I have no idea whether I will be like mine or not.'

'Don't be silly,' she said. 'Fathers don't count.'

'Mine will,' said Abe and then wondered why he had spoken with such conviction.

Alicia looked at him oddly. 'You can go back to sleep if you like, I have to keep driving; I think she can smell us if we stop in one place too long.'

Abe remembered the way she had lifted her head, scenting the air like a dog. Perhaps she could follow someone's trace. He thought of the films he'd seen with convicts wearing stripy clothes, wading through swamps, and the shouts of guards, and whistles in the distance, and closer, heavy throated barking: hound dogs closing in. That was Mrs Dunne.

In a way, the experience at Jack's house was even more disappointing than the others. The family were there all right. Jack himself went and knocked at the door. The coach had managed to pull up opposite so all the team crowded over to the right side and were peering through windows to see what would happen. Jack winked and then when the door opened he gave a wave before stepping inside. Except he wasn't invited inside. The door opened wider and Abe and the others could first see a young woman, maybe twenty-two or twenty-three years old standing there, asking questions as Jack waved his hands and vigorously nodded his cropped grey head; and then a man joined the woman, much older, possibly the same age as Jack himself. He was clearly cross and Jack began to back away. The door slammed. Jack stood on the top step for a moment before slowly turning. He crossed the road with his head down, oblivious to the traffic.

'What's the story, Jack?' called out Griffin as Jack came back on to the bus.

'They were, um, very nice,' he said and then quickly sat down beside Abe right up at the front and took out a large handkerchief and blew his nose.

Alicia watched him closely and Abe asked him whether he was all right.

'Yes, yes,' he said, shoving the handkerchief away, taking a deep breath and standing up again, 'I'm always all right, I'm Jack the lad, aren't I?' This last bit was thrown out to his friends at the back.

'Whoah, Jack,' whooped his pals.

'What did they say?' asked Alicia. 'What did those people at the door say to you?'

'Oh,' he said carelessly, 'they said I was dead and that the police had already been on to them about some fraudster chappie trying to worm his way into families, trying to get his hands on their money. They told me to shove off or they'd call the police.'

Abe felt sorry for the team's joker. 'Who was it at the door, Jack?' he asked.

'My younger brother,' said Jack. 'Knew him straight off. Seemed awfully nice really. Considering, you know. The girl called him Dad. Must be my niece.' He took out his handkerchief and studied it in a puzzled fashion for a moment before putting it away again. 'They wouldn't tell me anything about my parents.'

He made his way back to his seat and Abe heard him saying: 'Oh no, they just need a bit of time, need to get used to the idea of old Jack coming back.'

Between them, Abe and Alicia decided that the best they could do was to take the team to breakfast, which would use up the last of the money, then dump them in Hyde Park where they could play their first game of football for sixty years while Abe and Alicia tried to cash more money using her mother's card. Then they would see if Abe's mother's flat was clear. If it was, they could phone all the other families, just to check whether even one of the eleven would make it back home. And if all that came to nothing, said Alicia, which she was certain it would because her mother seemed to be one step ahead of them, impersonating the police and phoning Jack's family and most likely all the other families too, then Abe would have to think of what to do next because she was beginning to feel tired. She yawned.

Abe didn't say anything but he had another reason for going to his mother's flat—he never could quite bring himself to call it 'home'. She must have a birth certificate for him hidden away somewhere. He'd need it, wouldn't he, to prove to the Egyptian embassy that his father was Egyptian so they would then have to give him a passport and help him.

They found a McDonald's and Abe led the team in and did his best to explain how to order. Alicia wouldn't come in. 'Cow meat,' she said. 'Haven't you ever seen a cow, Nasfali? Couldn't possibly eat one of those things. They have hoofs and udders.'

'You mean you don't like McDonald's,' said Abe, smiling.

'I don't think I like very much,' she said, and closed her eyes.

Inside the yellow and orange plastic restaurant there was chaos, a bedlam of shouted questions and laughter, while increasingly irritated young servers tried to explain the difference between a MacChickenSandwich and a Big Mac and regular fries.

'One is a burger, sir.'

'What's a burger?'

'It's a sort of bun in a box.'

'Like a tea bun?'

'No, not really; more like a sandwich.'

'Like that MacChicken thing.'

'Not quite.'

Abe untangled the muddle and shepherded them back to the coach where there was then the serious sound of slurping and chomping and belching and general approval for the food.

While the team ate, Alicia drove them to the park and nosed them into a row of empty parking spaces close to Alexandra Gate. 'Wasn't that a bit of luck,' she said.

'Do we have money to pay for all those meters?' said Abe.

'It's not our coach,' said Alicia, 'so we won't have to pay anything.'

Once the eating was over, Abe suggested a game of football.

Of course they didn't have a football, but Alicia managed to procure one from an arguing family, who trailed off after their steaming mother, wailing that they hated her.

'It's the same all over,' observed Alicia. 'Families are just not designed to get on.'

'Why were they all so cross?'

'Because I have their football, and don't you dare criticize me.'

'I wouldn't dream of it,' said Abe, and he wouldn't either.

The pair left the team flying up and down a practice pitch and made their way to the nearest cashpoint.

'Fingers crossed,' said Alicia sliding in the card and tapping out the number. But instead of seeing a list of choices come up on the screen, there was the face of Mrs Dunne glaring out at them. She was so close and so real that Abe jerked backwards and Alicia had to grab his arm to stop him toppling back into the road.

'I know where you are,' said Mrs Dunne, 'so just wait and I shall come and get you.'

'And if we don't?'

The machine hiccuped, the image faded and was replaced with 'Out of Order'. Alicia's mouth twitched slightly, her version of a smile as Abe now recognized. 'A pity about the card,' she said. 'It's up to you now, Nasfali.' She suddenly released his arm, as if embarrassed. 'I'm skint.'

'Is your mother trapped in that broken machine?'

'If only.'

'Never mind,' said Abe, with a confidence he did not feel, 'I'll think of something.' After a moment's pause, and with Alicia waiting patiently, he said, 'We'll go this way.'

TEN

Number 23B Ennismore Gardens was a spindly building squeezed between expensive town houses smug with fresh paint and fat cars anchored like so many yachts in the 'Residents' Only' berths that lined the square. No one sat in the gardens in the middle of the square; no one walked on the pavement.

'Cheesy,' remarked Alicia, as the main door swung behind them.

'You think so?' said Abe. He had never really thought about where he lived. 'It is quiet,' he agreed, 'but we are near the park which is . . . '

'Nice?' offered Alicia.

'Yes.' He wasn't convinced that Alicia had much time for parks. She didn't seem the type. 'Do you think I sound a snob?' He held open the lift door for her and then clanged it shut.

'Doesn't matter what people sound like, Nasfali, does it?'

'But it matters where they live?'

She sniffed. 'Sometimes.'

The lift was one of those old-fashioned ones with an expanding grille door that you look through as you go up or down, seeing the inner wall of the building sliding past. It stopped on the third floor and there was Abe's home: a maroon door. Alicia studied it closely, running her hand over the surface and peering at some of the little scratches in the paintwork. 'Hm,' she said. 'It seems all right.' She sounded doubtful. 'Does it need a key?'

'Of course,' said Abe. 'Be a bit easy to break in otherwise, wouldn't it.' He paused and then grinned down at the key in his hand. 'Which is exactly what we are doing, really.'

'It doesn't count, breaking into your own house.'

'Have you broken into someone else's?'

She shrugged.

'So you haven't done absolutely everything have you, Miss Alicia Dunne?' he said triumphantly. 'Have you? Now I shall provide us with a telephone, so that we can, in safety, phone all the remaining families of the team, and I shall also supply us with sundry amounts of cash.' Sundry was a good word. The Latin teacher had used it the other week and Abe had thought it sounded important.

'OK,' said Alicia. 'That's good. Planning is good. You're the one who let them out; you're the one who's responsible for getting them home.'

'No,' said Abe. 'It was your mother who trapped them in the photograph, so you're responsible.'

'Half responsible.'

'Done,' said Abe.

'Is that what they call haggling?' she asked.

'Of course,' and with a flourish, pushed open the door. 'Please enter,' he said.

'You're sure it's safe?'

'Of course.'

She lifted her chin, straightened her shoulders and stepped past him, took one step and then stopped with a gasp. 'It's not human!'

Well, of course the apartment wasn't human, apartments tend not to be, though it was more peculiar than even the surprised Alicia suspected. She was overwhelmed by the razor-sharp neatness of everything. The front door opened into a sitting room where it looked as if no one had ever sat: surfaces gleamed, cushions swelled with silky exactness, and everything seemed so . . . balanced. What she saw on the left of the room was mirrored on the right, and back again, because there seemed to be mirrors everywhere, reflecting images to and fro. There was her face, there and there and there and there and there. Abe was so used to it, he didn't notice.

Alicia, catching sight of her own panicky white face,

endlessly repeated, felt dizzy. Too many straight lines. Her pale face first turned pink and then red, crimson, like her mother's did sometimes.

'Yes,' said Abe, 'it's a bit boring, isn't it.' Then he saw her and caught her arm. 'Are you all right? No, you're not, are you? This way, come on.' He led her into his room and sat her on the edge of his bed while he hurried into the kitchen, poured a glass of water, automatically wiped the sink and surface dry, and hurried back to her.

'Brilliant,' she said. 'Close the door, Nasfali, would you. Just for a minute.'

He did as she asked and Alicia visibly relaxed. His room with all its pictures of the desert, pyramids, the giant sphinx, the bustling streets of Cairo, and the wide, blue Nile was a different world to the rest of the apartment. 'That's better,' she said. 'Just wasn't ready for it, but I'll cope in a sec. It's the way your mum has it all sorted, you know. My mum is bad, obsessive, everything controlled; your mum is way worse though.' She shook her head. 'Way worse. Poor Nasfali. No wonder you're such a freak.'

'I'm not a freak!'

'It's a compliment, Nasfali.'

'Is it?'

'It means you're different; not one of the drones but not one of *them* either.'

'I'm not that different,' said Abe stubbornly. He hunted through his pockets for the paper on which he had scribbled all the names and addresses that the team had given him. 'What's a drone anyway?'

'Boys in the school, my dad, people in the street, students at my college, teachers, policemen, models, everyone who's not like my mum, or like your mum.'

'Oh.' He picked up the phone. Was it a good thing to be different? So different? He looked at the list. He didn't feel that different; just not English, not British.

Behind him, he heard Alicia taking another sip of water. 'Do you really want to be a drone, buzzing around, doing what you're told, ending up like my dad, or worse?'

'No,' he said, 'I won't end up like anyone in this country.'

'No, I know, because you're different. And you can thank your lucky stars you are because otherwise you would end up like your mother.' She pulled a face. 'I'm terrified I'll end up like mine.'

'You could never look like her!' Abe spluttered.

She looked up, startled by his vehement exclamation. Then took out a large spotted handkerchief and blew her nose loudly. Was she laughing at him, he wondered? But when she spoke she was her usual businesslike self. 'Let's get on with it, Nasfali. I don't think we've got much time.' She sniffed. 'They're close. I'll do the phoning if you give me the list and you go and find some money.'

He handed her the list of names and addresses. 'Nasfali,' she said, reaching for the telephone, 'are you serious about going to Egypt?'

'Yes.'

'Do you have a passport?'

'I don't know.'

'No, you won't have one. Where would your mother keep her important things?'

'Her room.'

'Find your birth certificate. You'll need it.'

'Yes, I know.'

'And some money.'

'Yes.'

As he hurried out of the room he heard her saying: 'Oh, hello, the name is Pike and the address . . . '

Money? The chrome and black thin chest by the front door often had cash in it. Abe opened it and found one, no, two notes and small change. He scooped it into his pocket. Not much, but it would help.

He froze suddenly. What was that? He shivered. It was like an icy fingertip on the back of his neck.

'Nasfali?' Alicia was calling him from the bedroom. 'What's the matter? Did you hear something?'

'Yes. No. I don't know. I felt something, that's all.'

'I think they're in the building, Nasfali. Not my mother but maybe yours.' Her voice changed. ' . . . Please. Jissop. Could you? I've two more names after this. If you could hurry . . . thank you.'

His mother in the building! What would she do if she found him there, and with Alicia Dunne? It would be the end of everything, that was for sure. 'Oh please.' He gritted his teeth. 'Please. Just three minutes. Please.'

He half closed his eyes and stood stock still, concentrating. Around him, the air seemed charged with electricity; his skin tingled, in his ears he could hear a faint humming sound. He lifted his left arm, and stretched out his hand and, still with his eyes half closed and facing the front door, he edged sideways. The tingling became sharper, little needles around his fingernails.

He had it, he knew he had it. There it was—the door to her room! He quickly slapped the palm of his hand against the mirrored surface and yelped. It was so cold, it burned like ice. But instead of pulling his hand away he pushed, and the door swung open.

'Suffocating sphinxes!' he whispered. How could it be like this? Dirt. Damp. A worm-eaten chest of drawers with clothes spilling out. Wallpaper, thickly striped in red and black with embossed figures peering through the stripes, but all peeling and scabbed with stains. There was no carpet on the cold stone floor and no light from the heavy wood shutters over the window. Opposite him was a heavily canopied four-poster bed. Moth-eaten drapes and yellowing sheets. How could this be hers?

The air was icy sharp. With every breath, he felt little spikes in his throat and the humming had screwed itself up into an angry scratching whine. 'No time,' he found himself muttering. 'No time.' It was hard to think with that noise. He was about to step back, just go for the money, grab Alicia and run for the park. He knew his mother was close. But he also knew that this was where she would keep hidden all that was most precious, all that she didn't want anyone else ever to see. This was where he had to look for his birth certificate.

Not the bed. No. The drawers? No. Confusion and decay everywhere. And he could find nothing to do with him.

He was beginning to panic. How could he ever escape? How could he go to Egypt, if there were no papers to prove his father was Egyptian? How could he travel, if he had no passport? How could he find his father or his father's family, if he had no name? What could he do? Just run, he and Alicia, delivering the team to whatever homes still existed. And then what? There was no then what, was there? Mrs Dunne, his mother, and all those other smart successful witches would find them. He would be brought back to Prackton Hall. Mrs Dunne would snap her fingers and he would find himself trapped in a nowhere world, framed and on a wall, staring out on to the long corridor.

The whine twisted into a thin squealing. He pressed his hands over his ears and sank down on to the edge of the bed. Accidentally he sat on part of the canopy which tore away and collapsed over his head, making him cough. The squealing sharpened. He had to get out.

And then it suddenly dawned on him. Here. Where he was sitting. If there was anything to find it was here. Frantic, he patted the bed; yanked up the mattress, stripped away the remaining drapes from the canopy. Nothing. He hurled aside the pillows.

And there, where his mother laid her head, was a box, quite small, about six inches square, and about half that in depth and there were other things there too: trinkets, a bracelet, a leather-bound notebook, and photographs. He flicked open the notebook. Yes! Tucked inside the cover were two certificates: the writing was Arabic. This had to be what he was looking for. He slipped them back into the notebook for safekeeping and jammed that into his pocket. What about the box? Should he keep it? Of course. It had to be important but it wouldn't open. The squealing was now so loud his hands trembled. His legs felt numb. He tried to stand and wobbled helplessly.

'Nasfali! Nasfali, come out of there. Now!' Alicia was framed in the doorway. Her hands pressed over her ears, just as his had been. Her face was in shadow because of the brightness of the sitting room behind her, but he could hear the fear in her voice and it jolted him up on to his feet. 'Come on!'

He shoved himself away from the bed and, still feeling wobbly, he lurched in a broken run across the room.

'They're here.' She had to shout to make herself heard against the ear-splitting squeal. 'We've got to go.' She tugged at his arm. 'Did you get money? We've got to have money. Did you get any?'

'Yes.' He pulled the door to his mother's room shut. The noise, though still bad, had decreased slightly and he found that his sense of balance was restored; he could move all right.

They ran out of the room, pulling the front door shut behind them. They could hear the lift whirring slowly up to them. 'Stairs,' said Abe. They clattered down to the next floor, and then ducked back out of sight and held their breath as the lift passed them. Abe could see his mother, still as a statue, staring through the grille, and two other figures behind her. 'This way.' He pushed through a door marked 'Fire Exit' and scrambled down an external iron staircase that led into a narrow yard which, in turn, led into a mews.

'Did you see her?' panted Abe, as they ran down the mews and towards the main road. 'Did you see that look on her face? I think she might do something horrible if she catches us.'

'Yes, Nasfali, that's what witches do. Horrible is what they are best at. Come on—we've left the boys too long as it is.'

Eleven

Traffic thundered by in a solid wall of double decker buses and fat black cabs and the lights seemed to take forever to change. Abe kept glancing back over his shoulder, at any moment expecting to see his mother or Mrs Dunne bearing down on them. 'They'll smell we were in the apartment. I know they will.'

'Yes,' said Alicia, her eye fixed on the lights, 'but they won't smell us out here. Too big; too many people. Go!' she suddenly shouted as the lights changed and the traffic stopped, and together they ran, weaving their way through pedestrians bent on crossing in the opposite direction to them, Alicia behind, running clumpily in her black boots. Through the park gate they ran, over the sandy drive used by horse riders, past children playing and couples walking, and nearly smack into a tall tanned young woman in shiny shorts gliding swiftly along on roller blades.

'Whoah! Sorry!' Abe blurted, as the young woman swizzled round in a tight spin. He glimpsed angry eyes and a tight-lipped look and then she was gone. He stopped and stared after her. 'Did you see that? She looked like mother. Are you all right?'

Alicia was bent over, her hands on her knees, catching her breath. 'Yes,' she said crossly and then, 'No, she didn't.'

Abe wasn't listening. He was scanning the green space that led up to the gate and the main road for the witches. But how could you tell them apart from anyone else? They wouldn't look out of place behind the handbag counter in Harrods; they wouldn't look out of place anywhere where there was money and smart business people. But they wouldn't come in one big group, would they? There had only been three in the lift. Perhaps the others had been downstairs. A flock of witches. Or maybe it should be a fright of witches. Yes . . .

'Coven,' said Alicia. 'It's called a coven.'

'What?' Abe turned, startled. 'How did you know what I was thinking?'

She didn't even look up. 'Because you were muttering to yourself.'

'Oh.' He kept looking around them. People. People everywhere. He and Alicia were too exposed. They should gather up the team and move on quickly. Supposing it was Lakin who found them, Lakin, the enormous greasy chef, with all those lookalikes. How had she done that, made him multiply? 'Come on,' he said, 'we can hide behind those trees.'

Alicia groaned but followed after him across the twenty or so yards to a stand of thick-trunked plane trees. 'They can make you do that, I think,' she said when she'd caught up, her hands squeezing in at her waist, trying to ease her stitch. 'Make you see them everywhere. It only works when you're scared though. It's a witch thing.'

'I am never frightened,' said Abe, and then catching the look she gave him, added, 'Maybe a bit, just sometimes.'

'Like now?'

He nodded.

'Well, we're OK for the moment. There's no sign of them.' She slid down until she was sitting, her legs stuck out in front of her. 'What was that, Nasfali, in your mum's place? You looked like someone had plugged you into the national grid. You were all over the place. Had you never been into your mum's room before?'

Abe shook his head.

'That's it then. Bit of a shock when you find out what they're really like. You know: action plans, colour co-ordinated sitting room, you name it. But at the back of it all, it's a mess. They just keep it hidden.'

'Is that what hell's like?'

Alicia rubbed her nose. 'Don't know, but I think it's sick, all that pretending.'

All his life, it had been rules: leave no mess and tidy up and polish his shoes, and keep out of the way, and never never go into his mother's room. And he had never wanted to, not till today. He gripped the box tight in his hand. He didn't care that where she really lived was a filthy den. He didn't care. She could pretend as much as she liked. He was never going back.

'I'm on the outside,' said Alicia.

'Sorry?'

'I'm the same on the outside as I am on the inside. Just wanted you to know that.'

He looked at her carefully. What did she mean? That she had rings and things inside her?

'That's why I can't ever be like her and the others.'

'Oh,' said Abe. 'I see.' Alicia said weird things. But that was all right. Perhaps she would come to Egypt with him. She had said she might. 'How many of the families did you manage to contact?' he asked.

She shook her head.

'None?'

'None. They're all ours, Nasfali.'

'Out of the whole eleven, not one family.'

'What did you expect?'

'I thought maybe one. Maybe more.'

'You saw what happened to Jack, didn't you?'

'Mm, I don't know how they didn't recognize him.'

'Because the families think they're dead, Nasfali, all of them and over sixty years ago. I got through to two families on the phone and you know what I found out? That in 1942 there was a tragic accident, on the train going down to Brighton from London. A single bomb. No German bomber sighted or anything but the train blew up and all the team were on it.' She pushed herself up from the ground. 'Let's move. They're over that way.'

'But we know that's not true,' said Abe, finding it hard not to keep spinning around every two seconds to check whether a fat chef lookalike wasn't about to grab him by the scruff of the neck.

'Pike's sister told me that story, and when I said her brother was alive, she just said, "Who is this?" Then: "I shall call the police if you ever try to call again." Then she put the phone down on me. Nice, don't you think? I discovered that Mum had sorted it. Even when she was that young, she could do things like that—make everyone believe that the team she'd trapped in a photograph had all died when that train exploded. Had it reported in the national papers and everything. What a cover up. Powerful or what?'

They left the shelter of the trees and hurried down towards the end of the Serpentine, and then crossed to the far side where they had left the team and where they could now see a small crowd round one of the improvised pitches, and a lot of cheering and shouting going on. Griffin and company having the time of their lives and the crowd were loving them.

Abe and Alicia threaded their way through a group of youngish Americans in baseball caps and floppy-joe T-shirts, in time to see fat Roberts spin past a player half his age, slip the ball across to Jack who cracked it straight into the corner of the goal, leaving the goalkeeper gawping.

'Yay! See that little guy go.'

'Hammer out of hell,' said another. 'Maybe we should take 'em on?'

The team cheered. Griffin skipped over to Roberts and flicked his ear. Then spotting Abe and Alicia he gave a grin and the thumbs up.

'They don't look dead, do they?' said Abe.

'No,' agreed Alicia, 'but looks can be deceiving, can't they?'

The game started up again.

'I don't think that that train blew up. I think it's what you said. I think she can make people believe things. Maybe if we could prove that incident never happened then those families would have to listen to us. Shouldn't we get them away from here? All these people. Your mother or mine could be here any second . . . '

She gripped his arm. 'Nasfah. Wake up. It was a war. Is there going to be a record of every accident that happened then? No. The only way they go back to their families is if you could turn the clock back. So just forget it. You have to think of something else.'

'We,' corrected Abe. 'You agreed that it was "we".'

'All right, *we* have to think of something. How much money did you grab?'

On the pitch, the opposing team had clearly had enough of being humiliated by these elderly unfit looking men. They had grabbed possession of the ball by, it seemed to Abe, giving Stokely a savage jab in the ribs that left him winded and doubled over, and had launched a swift attack. Now the whole team, all fit young men in their twenties, were streaking down the pitch in their shiny team shirts looking grim faced and ready for business.

'Here!'

'Pass!'

'Smack him, Carlos.'

The crowd booed as Gannet, who had attempted a slightly ungainly sliding tackle, was bowled clean over and trampled by two of the opposition.

'Those are some mean guys!' exclaimed the American beside Abe.

'Do you know who they are?' asked Abe.

'Who, the old guys? No idea but they're some dream team, man.'

'No,' said Abe, 'the others.'

'Them? Oh, they're the Brazilians. They sure don't like getting caned.'

'Are they professionals?' asked Abe, his brain beginning to tick a little faster. If his team were doing that well against a pro bunch, then maybe, maybe, there really could be some business venture on the near horizon.

'Naw. Embassy team. Whole bunch of us play out here Saturdays. See over there, look, you got the French, the Saudis, Italians, Egyptians . . . You name it, everybody wants to play football. Heck, we do too, and it's not even American football!'

On the far side of the pitch, there were clusters of people watching, mostly young men and women in shorts, tracksuits, and sweatshirts who looked as if they might have been playing themselves a little earlier. But there was one small group who caught Abe's eye. They were smartly dressed. At their centre was an elderly man, grey haired and bearded, wearing a long flowing Arab robe. He was watching the game intently, gesticulating with one hand and clutching a slender walking stick in the other with which he stabbed at the air in excitement.

'The Egyptians,' said the young American, when Abe asked who they were. 'You know, these old guys are good,' he said. 'They're sure giving the Brazilos a run for their money, but I tell you we don't play the Brazilians, they're rough.'

Indeed they looked it. Gannet was only just getting to his feet when Abe saw Bittern get shouldered so hard that he went flying off into the crowd on the far side of the pitch and sank down onto his knees. They'd all end up in hospital if he didn't stop it. He made a move, but Alicia grabbed him. 'No,' she said, 'wait. Wait and see.'

The Brazilians were moving down in a formation of four passing the ball to each other, shouldering any of Abe's team who came near them out of the way. They skirted Thomas and Chivers, passed across to the centre and so there was just Jissop and Pike, the full backs, and Jack rubbing his hands together in goal.

'Team!' roared Griffin suddenly. 'Scissors!'

For a moment Abe thought that the strain had perhaps been too much for the skipper and he had cracked but then to his astonishment, and the complete bewilderment of the Brazilian team, all the elderly men on the pitch, all those still standing that is, suddenly leapt into the air and did a scissor jump and while their opponents hesitated, they then squealed like pigs and changed places with each other. As they did so, impassive looking Jack loped straight up to the four attackers, scooped up the ball and hurled it overarm halfway back down the pitch. The Brazilians were so busy shrugging their shoulders and calling out to the rest of their team that they hardly noticed what had happened and by the time that they had, the ball had bounced off Gannet's head and landed right in front of Jonson who instantly passed it to Roberts, who scored again.

The crowd cheered and laughed; the Brazilians scowled. But then, when Griffin, who seemed to have suffered injuries like all the others, limped over to shake hands with their skipper they appeared to relent. They shrugged again and smiled, and patted their elderly opponents on the shoulder. 'Bravo,' they said, 'you have good tricks—we like that. Maybe you have the spirit of Ronaldo.'

'And who's he,' muttered Bittern, cradling his left arm which had taken the force of his heavy fall, 'the bishop of Bromley or something?'

'No, no,' said one of the Brazilians who had overheard him, 'not a big shop but the great footballer, Ronaldo. But much younger than you,' and he gave Bittern a 'friendly' punch on his sore arm. 'Oh,' he exclaimed when Bittern winced. 'So very sorry,' and his eyebrows hooped in mock distress, and then he sauntered off.

'Maybe,' said their skipper to Griffin, 'maybe we beat you next time. A friendly, hey!' and he grinned, long white teeth against olive skin. He made Abe, who was standing on the edge of the circle of players, think of a shark, and sharks made him think of danger, and danger made him think of Lakin, and Mrs Delia Dunne. He clutched the box he'd grabbed from his mother's room, and looked around him. He caught Griffin's eye and shook his head.

'Another time,' said Griffin, 'when you've had a chance to practise, old chap.'

The Brazilian didn't answer. He merely snapped his fingers and then made a circling motion in the air, and his team pulled away, leaving the victorious but bruised Prackton eleven to plump down on to the grass for a rest.

'We should go,' Abe said to Alicia. 'I don't trust them.'

'Who?' Alicia had been talking to the two Americans who just happened to be standing beside them when they were watching the game. 'They just don't like being beaten. Typical men,' she sniffed.

'Maybe your guys would like to play our team?' said the American to Alicia.

Abe wasn't paying attention. He suddenly felt the temperature change. Cooler. 'We should go,' he repeated. The crowd had already begun to drift away. The Brazilian team appeared to be gathering their things, but to Abe's suspicious eyes were taking too long and they had somehow drifted into a loose circle round the team, Alicia, and him. 'Back to the coach,' he called across to Griffin.

Griffin nodded and beckoned to the others.

'How about it?' the American was saying. 'A little wager, what do you say? Jed,' he turned to his companion, 'don't you reckon we should play these guys and have a little bet on the side.'

'Sure.'

'No, I don't think so,' said Alicia. She too had started to look around.

'What?' Abe's mind was fizzing. There was something very wrong but he had suddenly caught on to what the Americans were proposing. Money? They had thirty pounds and some small change, of course they needed money. 'How much?' he said, his eyes all the time on the Brazilians. How come they all looked so alike? Fatter and larger than they had seemed when playing?

'Whaddya propose?'

Abe blinked and looked seriously at the man making the offer. He was tall, clean shaven, smiling easily— someone to be trusted? 'A thousand pounds,' said Abe abruptly.

'Whoee,' whistled the American. 'And you're their manager, are you?' He raised an eyebrow.

'Yes.'

'And you have that sort of dough, do you?'

'Of course. Well, we don't, but the team do,' said Abe.

'Yes,' said Alicia. 'Pots of money.'

'Excuse us.' The two Americans stepped back to confer.

Abe looked back to the Brazilians. It was happening again, just like in the club. Where there had been eleven smooth, fit looking Brazilian footballers, casually picking up bags, shucking off football boots, and slipping on trainers, there were now eleven barrel-chested Lakin lookalikes, sleeves rolled up, forearms flexing, stubby fingers itching to grab. Why were they waiting?

'Alicia.'

'Yes.'

'Why are they waiting?'

She shook her head. 'No idea.' With some relief, they saw the team heading across the grass to the road. The Lakins made no move to stop them. They stood motionless, facing the little group where Abe, Alicia, and the two Americans were. Who did they want?

'OK,' said the American, coming back rubbing his hands together, 'we can do a thousand. Same time tomorrow? Where are y'all staying?' He looked from Abe to Alicia. 'Are you guys in some kind of trouble?' His eyes followed theirs. 'Who are they? Geez, look like beef on the bone to me. What do you say, Jed?'

'Beef on the bone,' agreed Jed.

'So, what's the story?'

Alicia looked at Abe. 'Tell them, Nasfali.'

Tell them? Who would believe the truth? 'It is like this,' said Abe, and with a fluency that surprised even himself, especially since he couldn't tear his eyes from the watching Lakins, he made up a story about the team, how they all lived in a home for the mentally disturbed. 'Not bats,' Abe suggested quickly, 'a little . . . mm . . . confused maybe.'

'They think they are only twelve or thirteen years old,' added Alicia.

'Kind of weird,' nodded Jed. 'But they got money, you say.'

'Oh yes,' said Abe, 'very rich families and they want to play. They claim they were—are—a school team and . . . ' Abe found himself shivering. Something bad was getting closer. No, not it, *she* was coming. She was close. 'Alicia,' he said, 'you must go. Please. Please. Take this.' He thrust the small box into her hands.

She frowned. 'Where?'

'We can put you up,' said the American. 'We can put your coach right bang in the embassy coach park and there ain't nobody can touch you there.'

'That's good,' said Abe through chattering teeth. 'Now go, please,' he urged Alicia. 'I'll follow.'

'Do you know what you're doing?'

She is concerned, thought Abe, that is good. He nodded. 'Yes.'

With the two Americans flanking her, Alicia headed towards the coach. The Lakins, Mrs Dunne's creatures, followed her. So it is her they want, thought Abe. But the Lakins kept their distance, as if they were frightened of coming too close. At one point Alicia, clearly irritated by them, spun round and shouted something that Abe couldn't quite hear but it made the eleven barrel-chested chefs stop dead in their tracks and fling up their arms as if to shield themselves from her. Yet as soon as she turned away, they began to follow again. It was like a rather horrid game of grandmother's footsteps, thought Abe, but at least there seemed a protective shield between her and them.

It made Abe wonder about her. What could she do, Alicia? She said she wasn't like Mrs Dunne and she wasn't, but maybe you inherit some things without knowing. He watched her reach the coach safely, and climb on, and the coach drive off. The Lakins seemed to hesitate, and then after a moment they jogged off after the coach. They would not be able to follow for long, surely. Abe let out a deep breath and, hugging himself from the cold, turned round.

'Hello, mother,' he said.

TWELVE

She stood very still, about five paces away, half in the shadow of a plane tree, her hands by her side, her chin tilted slightly so it was hard to tell whether she was looking at him or at something behind him. Her face was frost white in the softened light of the tree's shade.

'Hello, mother,' he said again, rubbing his hands up and down his arms, trying to get a bit of warmth into them. He wasn't frightened, not at the moment, just relieved that she was on her own. He wasn't even surprised at her materializing like this, not with what he had seen and heard in the last two days. She was a witch: he had seen her room; he had seen her with Mrs Dunne; but she wasn't with the terrifying Mrs Dunne now. She had come to find him on her own because she wanted to see him, not any of the others. He felt a momentary twinge of pity for Alicia; at least his mother wasn't a hag, no, of course she wasn't. She was perfect, in a frozen, unsmiling, and, well, perfect sort of way. And so, now he could say goodbye to her and that was only proper for she was, witch or not, his mother.

At his greeting, she shifted very slightly. The fingers of her right hand, he noticed, curled and then straightened, as if she were just waking up—except there she was, eyes open, and standing in the middle of Hyde Park. The cold eased.

'Did you really think you could run away?' Her voice was a low angry rasp, nothing like he had ever heard before. For some reason he thought of snake venom, and instinctively took a step backwards. 'You stupid, ignorant child.'

Before he could protest, or revise his idea that saying

goodbye was such a good thing, and that running away like a turbo-charged camel was exactly what he needed to do, her eyes had locked on to him and instantly his head felt as if it had been caught in a metal trap. This was not what he had expected. He couldn't shift or turn or step back, or avoid looking into her eyes which were now as grey and as cold as an empty winter road.

'How dare you touch my things?' She lifted her hand and for a moment he thought she was about to strike him. 'Do you know what you mean to me?' She kept her voice low, the anger controlled. 'I could extinguish you like this,' and she snapped her long pale fingers in his face. Instinctively he tried to jerk his head back but, of course, he couldn't. 'Thief,' she said. 'Thief. Give me back what you stole from my room.' She brought her face so close to his that he could feel her cold breath on his eyes. 'Give it to me, Ebrahim . . . ' She never called him that, never . . . 'or I will tear your heart out and feed it to my sister's dog.'

'I didn't steal anything.' Denial is always sensible. Anyway, he hadn't stolen anything, just a few pounds to feed the team. 'Just a little money . . . for food.' He felt himself draining down into those grey wintry eyes.

'I don't mean stupid money. From my room. From MY room!'

The box! It was the box she wanted, the little box. The one he thought might have the papers he needed that proved who he was, to prove who his father was. Why should she care so much? It wasn't precious; it wasn't gold or silver. His heart hammered his ribcage so hard it hurt and his mouth was so dry he could barely whisper: 'I don't have it.'

'Liar.'

'No.'

'Liar.'

But he wasn't lying. 'I have nothing of yours,' he said, which was true; Alicia had the box. Why was it so important to his mother? No, that didn't matter, what mattered was that if it was that important, then he had to hold on to it at all costs, for he had nothing else to bargain with.

She lifted her head and sniffed. 'She has it,' she said suddenly. 'She was there too; I smelt her. Well . . . ' She looked away from him, and he felt the grip on his head disappear. 'All running away,' she seemed to be speaking more to herself than to him now, 'but not for long, she'll have them and,' her gaze fixed on Abe again, 'and my dear sister will have you too unless you give me back what you have stolen.'

'I don't know what you mean,' said Abe. 'I don't want anything of yours so you can let me go.'

'You think I'll let you go?'

It had never occurred to Abe that she would be anything other than delighted. 'I want to go to Egypt. You must have known that.'

'Why?'

Why? Because it was obvious. Because of all the pictures in his room, the books from the library, the questions he had asked. Had none of that made any impression on her at all. 'Because of my father.'

The harsh rasp came back into her voice. 'He is dead. Completely dead.'

Abe shook his head. 'No.'

'Dead,' she repeated. 'Do you know what that means? Shall I show you. Do you want to see where your father is, where my dear sister will put you and those others when she catches up with me?'

No. He shook his head. He didn't want to see at all. He wanted to be so far away that there was a thousand miles of ocean between himself and her.

'This,' she said, catching his arm and holding it tight, 'this is where we put boys like you.' And he found himself staring into those dead grey eyes again, and the tree behind her, and the blue sky, and the long expanse of grass and winding paths with all those ordinary people, walking and cycling and feeding the ducks, faded into motes of dust, and all he was aware of was that pinching grip on his arm and her low harsh voice saying, 'Didn't you know, Ebrahim, that we never let go. Never. That everything is kept. Look, Ebrahim. What do you see now?'

He saw a vast and dismal cavernous space. It was as if London's underground had been stripped and trashed: the ground was broken rubble and dirt; a crudely levelled building site with no building. There were no steps or stairs, or rails or platforms or people, only this stumbling desolation stretching left and right as far as he could see. Behind and in front of him scuffed and cracked stone side-walls vaulted upwards, so that Abe felt rather than saw that there was no sky but a ceiling somewhere overhead, lost in the grey half light which made everything visible but indistinct.

He felt her tight grip on his arm. 'Well?' A voice without a body; a touch without a hand. Where was she? Was this hell? 'Is this where I shall store you, Ebrahim? Is that what you want? Like your stupid father.'

'No. Please.' His voice was flat, unrecognizable to his own ears. Dead. There was a taste of dust in his mouth. She couldn't leave him here, not here, this was worse than the team's fate, trapped behind glass. At least they had had each other. They hadn't been alone, like him, like his father. Dead. Was this being dead? Was this what she had done to his father?

She was lying, of course she was lying. All witches were nothing more than lies and viciousness. 'If you let me go,' he said, 'I can ask Alicia if she has what you are looking for. We didn't mean any harm . . . ' It wasn't hard to let his voice drop into a snivelling whine.

'Leave him there!' A different voice. A familiar voice. Mrs Dunne. His heart gave a panicky lurch. 'Unless,' her voice was right by his ear, her breath like rusty nails, 'unless he wants to tell us where the others are. Do you want to do that, Nasfali?'

'Do you, Ebrahim?'

'No, please!' He squeezed his eyes shut against the nightmare, but the voices were still there, urging him.

'Tell us, Nasfali. Tell us.'

Should he? It wasn't fair that he was here and he had been the one to release them. He cursed his bad luck that had led him to be standing there in the corridor on the very night that the team of 1942 had come out of the photograph. It wasn't fair.

'Give them back to us. I want them back.' Mrs Delia Dunne's words coiled dizzily round Abe's head. It was unfair. Why should they play their stupid football, and have their stupid jokes and . . .

'Yes, why should they have all the fun, Nasfali, and you here, Nasfali? It's not fair, is it . . . '

Perhaps it was the pinching grip on his arm, or the sickly sweet smell of Mrs Dunne's breath, or a deep core of common sense that Abe had in him that made him see that it wasn't fair for the team to be old men, nor for Alicia to have such a mother; that made him know deep in his heart that whatever they said they would never let him go. 'Go back,' he said suddenly. 'Go back to wherever you come from. Go!'

And, to Abe's astonishment, they went.

There was no pinching grip just above his elbow, no breath on his cheek, no oily voice cajoling in his ear. He was alone and that was good, but he was alone in that terrible place and that wasn't so good.

At least, he thought he was alone, because he could see nobody else there. And yet, he had a feeling he was not completely alone. What had his mother meant—stored, like his father? Had she trapped his father into somewhere like this? Were there other places like this? Did every witch have her own . . . cellar, like this, where she kept any child or adult who crossed her in any way?

He thought of his mother's terrible room, hidden away

behind the mirrors of their smart apartment; he remembered what Alicia had said of her own mother; and he wondered whether this horrible place was the real world for witches, from where they emerged, squeezing their way into the upper air, pretending to be ordinary people, gradually taking over; and when they had taken over, would the world become this?

He quickly looked around, straining his eyes: no one. But then he thought he could hear the faintest of sounds, a tiny, tiny whispering, or shuffling. What was it?

He took a few steps in one direction, his feet scuffling on the broken ground. Behind him, closer, that sound. It was whispering, wasn't it?

'Who are you?' His voice fell flat into the lifeless air and there was no answer. Even that whispering, if that is what it was, ceased. But that was wrong, because there was a kind of answer: at first, like the whispering, it was so faint he was unsure whether he was imagining it. But it was there, an alien feeling of distress and sadness. And although there was no one to be seen, Abe felt that trapped down here, invisible to him, were other people, perhaps the shadows of children who had lost themselves, as he himself was lost. The feeling of unhappiness rolled in round him like a tide. It was so easy to give in to it.

No!

No snivelling. He wiped his nose and wiped his eyes, and took a deep breath of the stale, dusty air and straightened his shoulders. He couldn't remember the last time he had cried, but it certainly hadn't done him any good, otherwise he would have remembered. Crying wasn't going to get him out of this place; and crying wasn't going to get him to Egypt. And crying wasn't going to help him find his father, or find out what happened to his father; crying wasn't going to impress Alicia.

It is better to do something than nothing, he thought, and so he began to walk, slowly because the ground was broken and awkward, and because he still felt heavy with sadness.

He walked and walked, for hours or minutes—time had no meaning—he could still see the same rubble and rubbish underfoot, the same grey light. He told himself he was in the desert, trekking along, across dune after dune, hoping that at each rise he would finally see the green land that edged the Nile, and the deep blue that was the great river itself.

'Nasfali!'

So vividly did he imagine that he was on this desert journey, his caravan of one, that he didn't at first hear the voice shouting out his name.

'Nasfali!'

The second time, he smiled, and waved to the imaginary figure, on the imaginary horizon, waving and beckoning him on, just over the next imaginary dune to the cool valley of the Nile.

'Nasfali!'

The third time he blinked and the grey rubble world settled around him again and he stopped.

'Don't stop. Hurry!'

And suddenly there was Alicia, running clompily across the rubble, her pink dress smeared with dirt, as if she had had to squeeze her way through and down into this underworld.

'Alicia! You are . . . '

'I know, like a big wind.'

'No, a great camel, a ship of the desert . . . '

'Give it a rest, will you, and put your skates on, the coach is now on a yellow line and we can't afford to get clamped.' She grabbed his arm and set off running back in the direction from which she had appeared and he ran along beside her.

'How do we get out? Is there a door?'

'No.'

He glanced across at her. Her face was set in a tight

frown, her brow furrowed.

'How did you find me, then?'

'Concentrated. It worked for me on my own.'

They kept running but nothing changed; no dunes, or rivers, or paths, or green. 'What are you concentrating on?'

'The coach. Think of the coach.'

Abe thought. He pictured it, tucked into the kerb, a traffic warden stalking towards it, Gannet's worried beaky face peering out from the door, the hooting of traffic, and Griffin behind him, shouting: 'Come on, you two!'

And the pavement was smooth and hard underfoot, and the traffic warden as they barged past him was solid, and his 'Oi, you, mind that,' was clearly audible, as was Gannet's 'Oh, thank goodness' and Griffin's 'Three cheers, lads, Jungle Jim is back!'

And Abe was too bewildered to mind as he slumped into the seat behind the driver or to register anything other than that it was the vision who had rescued him, and the vision who had only just this second let go of his hand, given him a smile—she smiled!—before grabbing the wheel and yanking the coach out into the stream of traffic.

'Where are we going?' he asked.

'What?' Griffin leaned over and grinned. 'Gave us a bit of the jitters, you disappearing like that.'

'Where?' Abe flapped his hand at the window.

'American embassy, don't you remember? You and Miss Dunne were talking to the chap. I say, I think he took a bit of a shine to her, you know,' and he winked.

'A shine?' He didn't think he wanted anyone taking a shine to Alicia. He half closed his eyes. At least this felt safe, for the moment. Shine, wasn't that what you did to lamps and then a genie popped out? Alicia was a bit of a genie the way she had popped out of nowhere and grabbed his hand. He let his eyes close and for ten minutes he slept.

THIRTEEN

When the tall black gates at the rear of the United States embassy swung shut behind the coach, Abe should have felt relieved. He should have felt safe. He should also have joined in with the team's full-throated 'For he's a jolly good fellow' when the young man who had chatted to Alicia at the football match stepped up into the coach and welcomed them to the land of the brave and the free. But he didn't. He peered out at the armed US marines who stood stony faced on either side of the entrance to the building; he glanced up at the mirror glass windows that reflected puffy clouds and a blue sky, and he wondered who was staring down at them. It seemed safe, but then he wondered whether anywhere could really be safe from Mrs Dunne and his mother.

'If you guys want to play ball, we got a pitch right here.' The American pointed across to a broad square of green on the far side of the enclosure. 'And if you get hungry, you just tell me and I'll get you burgers the size of which you will never have seen in your entire lives. No, no please,' he said holding up his hand as the team threatened to launch into another chorus of noisy and tuneless 'He's a jolly good . . . ' 'No, no reason to thank me; I am looking forward to the game, and I am looking forward to winning a little money from you guys.'

'You'll be lucky,' shouted Griffin. 'We haven't got a sausage.'

'I guess I'm not looking for sausages.'

'Haven't got a bean between us,' called out Bittern.

'No pocket money,' explained Stokely.

The young man cocked an eyebrow in surprise. 'Well, that ain't what this beautiful young lady said to me a little while back.'

'Of course we can bet,' said Alicia in her matter-of-fact way. 'Nasfali and I have the money sorted, don't we, Nasfali.'

'What? Oh, of course.' It wasn't Alicia who had said they could bet that sort of money; it had been him. Spur of the moment, of course. It hadn't occurred to him that the American might actually want to see their money.

'Three cheers for Miss Dunne,' shouted Jack. 'She's a lot more fun, than her mum.'

This produced raucous laughter, flailing fists, and flying socks.

'Miss Dunne's our mum!'

'Thank you,' said Alicia, 'that will do.' And it did.

'Gee, I don't know how you do that,' said the young man, who'd introduced himself as Bob, or was it Bobby. Abe hadn't been listening. He was neat and good looking and easy going.

'He's like cheese spread,' Abe kept saying to himself. 'Why doesn't Alicia tell him to go away?' But she didn't. In fact, she seemed to like his attention.

'These old guys are jest eating out of your hand. It's like you said, they're almost little kids. There's no real harm in them. And you reckon they'll be OK to sleep on the bus?'

'Well . . . ' began Alicia, 'they do need a rest . . . '

'They'll be very comfortable on the coach,' said Abe firmly.

Alicia looked at him curiously, gave a slight shrug, and said, 'We'll be fine, thank you.'

'You sure? I reckon we could get accommodation for y'all. I wouldn't say they pose a significant security risk.' He laughed and Alicia smiled at him. 'I mean they may be a little creaky but that's about it. Still, if you want them to stay right here, you're welcome. Now maybe if you could just do a little paper work, son,' he said addressing Abe. 'It's a bit of red tape, I guess, but we got to have names and signatures and all. Could you do that for me?' and he passed a clipboard to Abe and then immediately turned to Alicia again. 'Do you and your brother want to come inside? I can fix a guest room . . . ' and then Abe moved out of earshot. Brother? Did they look alike? Didn't the man have eyes? Couldn't he see? Unintentionally, he gave an Alicia-type sniff.

'Do you like my wizard signature?' Jonson looked up at Abe and smiled.

'Of course he does,' said Thomas, giving him an affectionate slap on the top of his gleaming bald head.

'Yes.' Abe nodded distractedly. Wizard? Magic. If only he could wave a wand . . . 'Now yours, Jissop.' The team chattered and signed, and gawped at the guards with their sleek M15 rifles. Abe collected the information, all the time glancing back up the coach where Bob was talking earnestly, and Alicia was nodding, and, it seemed to Abe, hanging on his every word.

'Here you are,' he said curtly, handing the clipboard back when he was finished.

'Thanks, pal.' Briefly Bob studied the list and then looked up. 'You two need to add your names.' Alicia took the pen and printed her name. Abe hesitated and then followed suit. He didn't know why but he didn't feel happy handing anything over to people they didn't know, no matter how friendly they seemed.

'Nasfali,' said Bob. 'So you guys aren't related.'

'No.'

'Not even English, hey?'

'Egyptian,' said Abe.

The young man's expression subtly altered. 'Is that right?' He tapped the pen against his teeth. 'Kind of out of place with these guys, aren't you?'

'What do you mean?'

'His mother is English,' said Alicia. 'He has an English passport and he goes to an English school. Is there a problem, Bob?'

121

'Yes, Bob,' said Abe, 'is there a problem? I should not like to be thought of as a problem.'

'Hey, steady there, Mr Egypt. I didn't mean to imply anything. I don't see any problems, but security can get a little twitchy, y'know.'

'I shall refrain,' said Abe coldly, 'from doing anything that might make anyone twitchy.'

'OK. OK. Tell you what, let me just check it out, will you?' And he ducked down out of the coach and they watched him pace over to the main building, giving what looked like a discreet no-go hand wave to the guard by the gate.

'Hm.' Alicia unscrewed one of the studs that peppered the top rim of her left ear, rubbed it on the hem of her pink dress and absently studied it. 'What's the matter with you, Nasfali?'

'Me!'

'You're prickly.'

'I am what I am.' He rather liked that; dignified.

'Are you jealous?'

'Jealous! Me? Of him?' He gave a scornful laugh. 'Suspicious would be more like it.'

'Of Bobby?'

Was she teasing him? He decided to ignore her deliberately familiar use of his name. 'Him, yes, but not just him, all of them, all of this.' He gestured at the high embassy walls, the blank-faced guards. 'It's like a trap.'

She pulled a face, and then shrugged. 'And you're only half Egyptian, anyhow.'

'I feel Egyptian.'

'You don't even speak Egyptian.'

'Arabic.'

'You don't even speak Arabic.'

'I'll learn.'

She sniffed, and Abe bit his tongue to stop himself from saying anything.

Griffin poked himself forward. 'When's tucker?' he

enquired. 'We're getting peckish, you know, and the chaps are v. keen on those burger whatnots.'

Abe ignored him. 'I think we should leave,' he said to Alicia. 'I'm not happy about being here.'

'Are you barmy!' exclaimed Griffin. 'Tucker! Match! Big match! Big bet! Miss Dunne,' he appealed to Alicia, 'what's he talking about?'

'Just go and sit down, Griffin,' she said. 'Food will be along soon. Trust us.'

Griffin beamed at her.

'Griffin!'

'Course, Miss Dunne. Absolutely.'

The chirpy captain backed away, his ear tips glowing, and was tripped by Pike. He landed with a thump on his backside, and then Bittern got up and accidentally fell on top of him. Within seconds there was a ridiculous bundle of old men in the aisle, whooping with laughter, and somewhere underneath them all Griffin letting out yelps. 'Ouch, you're breaking my arm!'

'I'm serious,' said Abe. 'I don't think we are safe here.'

'Of course we're not safe,' she said, 'we're not safe anywhere. But if you can convince Bob that we do have a thousand pounds to bet, we could end up winning enough to feed the boys for a few weeks.'

'Or fly them to Cairo.'

She pulled a face. 'Maybe. Not sure.'

'Not sure if that would be enough money to pay for flights, or not sure that it's a good idea to get them out of the country, or not sure if you want to see a bit more of Mr Bob?'

'Both. And if I want to talk to Bob that's my business. I do what I want, Nasfali. That's it. You have no business to get jealous.' And she shot him such a sharp look he felt as if he'd been stung.

'I'm not jealous.'

But he was jealous. That's exactly what he was. 'If you want to talk to that person, why should I mind? My name is Nasfali and he is "a little twitchy" about Arabs. Talk to him. Maybe I should go somewhere that isn't "twitchy". Maybe I should go to another embassy. How about that?' He was being ridiculous. He knew it but he couldn't stop himself.

'You could,' she said. 'It would be running out on us, of course.'

'What do you mean? You don't need me. You drive the bus. You got us here. It's you and the team your mother is after, not me. It's nothing to do with me. All this,' he waved his hands about, exasperated that a great adventure had slithered into a squabble, 'all this spells and things. If your mother hadn't made me stand in the corridor . . . '

'Exactly,' said Alicia. '*You* were the one. I just agreed to help, remember?'

He remembered the way she'd taken control in the kitchen and immediately the team were scuttling about doing exactly what she told them. He remembered hoping that she would come with him to Egypt. Well, maybe he should start looking out for number one. He always had in the past, hadn't he? 'Can I have my box, please?' he said.

She shrugged and reached down beside the driver's seat and handed it over.

'Did you open it?'

She shook her head. 'No. And I'd be careful if I were you.'

'Why? It's just a box. Why shouldn't I?'

'Your mother had it hidden, didn't she? So it was important to her. Don't you think,' she said, speaking patiently, as if having to explain something to a dim child, 'she might have a protective spell on it, perhaps. Had you thought of that, Nasfali?'

No. He was beginning to suspect that he wasn't very good at thinking of things. He stared glumly at his reflection in the window.

A moment later he felt a touch on his arm. 'We're the same, you and me, don't you see?' she said softly. 'Don't you get it yet?'

He didn't. He would never wear a ring in his eyebrow or in his nose. And she was a girl. A vision.

'Your mother and mine are witches. And we're . . . I know, cousins.' She shrugged. 'More than that . . . we're witches' brats, Nasfali. That's what they call us. And I don't want to be. I never have. I want to be my own person, and so do you, don't you? If we stick together we have a chance. I think we do anyway. And we can maybe help the boys, too. I've been thinking about them but if you just want to look out for yourself . . . '

How did she so often know what he was thinking? He stared at her, wondering for the first time whether he could trust her.

'Don't stare.'

'I'm not.' Of course he trusted her and he did want her to come to Cairo with him, more than he dared admit, though he didn't think she would, not now. And he wanted her to help him open the box, just in case there was a spell, but maybe he shouldn't ask now, not yet. 'What do you want me to do?'

She smiled. 'Find a way of convincing Bob that we can bet that thousand pounds, that would be a help. Can you do that?' She gave him that tilted-head look. 'Clever, scheming Nasfali? Can you do that while I organize food for the team. Here's Bob coming back; I'll keep him out of your hair. How's that? Will you do it?'

'Of course.'

She stepped down off the bus and skipped clumpily towards the young man, who, Abe noted, smiled and nodded as she talked at him. Then the two of them turned and went back into the building, the young man lightly holding her arm, guiding her. Abe sat back in his seat and pulled the money he had taken from his mother's apartment out of his pocket and laid it on his knee. Thirty pounds in notes: one ten and one twenty, and some change. Loaves and fishes, that's what Jesus did, didn't he? That was a kind of magic. Maybe there were all kinds of magic, not all bad. He closed his eyes and concentrated on the twenty pound note, multiplying it in his imagination into a thick little stack of notes, totalling a thousand pounds: crisp, neat as a deck of cards. He opened his eyes and there was the money: thirty pounds and some change. 'That's it!' he exclaimed. 'Easy.'

When Alicia returned with Bob, the two of them carrying bags of burgers for the team, Abe had a quiet word with her while Bob was dispensing the food. 'I'll be an hour,' he said. 'Will he let me back into the embassy?'

'You will come back?'

'Yes, but will you help me open this then? I think it might . . .'

' . . . Have something to do with your father?'

He nodded.

'You think he's still alive?' She took the box back and held it in her palm, as if weighing it. Then she quickly gave it back. 'We'll see.' Bob was coming back up the aisle to them, the team happily chomping on their burgers, their chins greasy with juice. Abe stepped down from the bus and let Alicia do the talking.

Twenty minutes later Abe was in W. H. Smith on Oxford Street, spending ten of the precious thirty pounds. With the bag tucked up under his arm, he found himself a quiet corner of a waitress service café in Selfridges, bought himself a toasted ciabatta sandwich and set to work.

Exactly one hour later, he rang the bell on the gate. The guard nodded him through and Abe walked quickly across to the bus.

The team, stuffed with beefburgers, were talking quietly; Alicia up at the front on her own was busy scribbling into a little notebook. 'Well,' she said. 'Do you have anything to show me?'

Abe opened the bag he was carrying and let her peek in.

'Mmm.' She gave him a thoughtful look. 'Clever,' she said.

'Maybe I have a talent,' said Abe modestly. He lifted out the wad of notes, crisply held together by a paper tape, just like you get in the bank. 'Can you stop him from looking closely at it?'

'Of course.' She flicked the edge of the wad, and it flickered like a stack of notes would, but when she did it again, a little more slowly, it wouldn't take a witch to see that only the top note was real. 'Very neat,' she said. 'No magic?'

'Just a pair of scissors,' he said. 'Now, shall we open the box?'

FOURTEEN

'Not yet.'

Alicia sat beside him, sometimes frantically writing, sometimes sucking the end of her pencil. He had asked her what it was about, but she wouldn't say, at least, not offering anything more than a curt: 'Things.'

The bus, apart from a pool of light shining down on Alicia and Abe where they were sitting up at the front, was dark, the curtains drawn; the team, snuffling and snoring gently, were asleep. Abe turned the metallic box around in his hands. It lay hard, slim, and oddly heavy in the palm of his hand. 'You agreed.'

'I know. I just think we shouldn't try to right now. We don't know what we'll find.'

'Oh yes, like a demon or something!' he said, frustrated.

She looked at him as if that was exactly what she feared but her voice, when she answered, was cool. 'You know what I mean.' Then she took up the notepad she had resting on her knee and looked back over what she had written.

Abe gripped the box. He had to open it. He had to take the risk, because whatever was in there was something so secret that his mother had been willing to bury him alive in that terrible place just to get it back. Abe's fingers itched to open it but there was no latch or catch, or lock that he could pick.

He had to get Alicia's help. She could do things. Things happened around her. How else had she managed to find him and get him out of that terrible place where his mother had put him? And all those other little things too: the way the team automatically did what she asked, and the American embassy official, Bob, she had him eating out of her hand too. And her mother, Mrs Dunne, wanted and expected her to be a witch like her, didn't she? Alicia didn't want that but perhaps she was turning into one anyway, almost without her helping it or knowing it.

He sneaked a look at her. She didn't look different—a bit scruffier: the short pink dress was crumpled and stained, her boots were scuffed; but the rings were all there and her hair was still twisted into those pixy spikes.

'You're staring at me, Nasfali.'

'Sorry.' He quickly looked away. 'How did you know?'

'What?'

'How did you know how to get us out of that empty, horrible place?'

She looked puzzled, chewed the end of her pencil, and then rapidly scribbled more stuff into her notebook.

'You said for me to concentrate on the coach and then it was there.'

She frowned. 'Did I? Yes, I did, didn't I. Worked too, didn't it?'

'Yes.' He held the box in the palm of his hand. 'If we both concentrate on the box do you think we can open it?'

'I don't want to open it.'

'But we could.'

She took the box from him and looked at it. 'We could, but,' she added slowly, 'I think if we do that, they'll know, and they'll come and find us.' She handed it back to him. 'Put it away, Nasfali. We can always try later. When this is all over.'

'No!' She was completely wrong, completely, totally wrong. 'They're going to find us anyway, aren't they? And the only way we'll escape is by keeping moving, keeping a step ahead of them, until we can get out of the country.'

'We're safe here. They've got guards and there's the match. The money. We can try later, Nasfali, when this is over.'

'What do you mean, "this"?' She didn't answer. 'We're not safe, and I don't like the guards. Don't you remember in the club how the bouncers changed, just like that, and the same with that Brazilian football team? Nothing is safe any more. Don't you see, it's going to happen here. Sooner or later, your mother is going to sniff us out and then your Bob and all the guards will turn into Lakins and we'll be trapped. Look at the place; it's a natural prison. We have to keep one step ahead, Alicia.'

She pulled back the curtain and looked out into the darkness.

'And that's why I want to open this,' he continued, 'and that's why you have to help me. There's something powerful in here, something that might weaken her and help us, and I know, I just have a feeling . . . '

'That there's something to do with Cairo,' she turned back to him, 'or your father?'

'Yes.'

She sighed. 'OK. Close your eyes. Concentrate. Picture it. Picture the box. Can you? Can you see it, every detail?'

'Yes,' he breathed.

'How does the box open, Nasfali?'

'A lid lifts up.'

'Can you see the lid?'

'Yes.'

'Is it opening now?'

'Yes.'

There was the faintest click and then the lid flipped up. Both of them hesitated for a moment, half expecting some trick. Nothing happened: no smoke, no genie, no monster. So they peered in. All there was was an old photo, no more interesting than the others he'd seen lying scattered about in the chaos of her room, and some bits of official looking paper.

Abe picked up the photo. 'I can't even see who it's of,' he complained. Of course he couldn't; the image had been so scribbled over and scratched, it was hard to make out any of the face at all.

'It's you,' said Alicia. 'Can't you tell?'

'No, I can't.' Odd. Very odd because as he looked, the scribbles seemed less severe, the picture fractionally clearer. 'No, it's not me. Someone older . . . '

'But very like you.' She paused and looked at him. 'Is it your dad?'

'My dad!' How peculiar that sounded. 'I don't know. My father?' He stared and stared at the image, as if somehow it could tell him everything. What had happened to him? And why, why had she kept the photograph like this. 'Why is it so messed up?' It was curious but even as he spoke, the image was definitely clearing.

'Nasfali, don't you understand what it is?' She closed her notebook. 'Basic bad magic. You want to hurt someone, and keep a hold on them, you do something like this.'

'Put them in a box and scribble and scratch on their face?'

'Don't be so literal, Nasfali. She has him trapped somewhere.'

'The scribbles?'

She hesitated. 'To hurt him, maybe even kill him. I'm sorry.'

'But not if the picture's still here—that must mean he's alive. He's somewhere; she has him trapped somewhere, like she was going to do to me. Is that what it is, Alicia? What do you think?' Without realizing it, he was gripping her arm. 'What do you think?'

'I think she must have hated him, Nasfali. Still does, that's why this is here. And yes, I'd say he is alive and yes, trapped in a witch's web. What did he do?'

Abe shrugged. 'I know nothing about him.'

'My father never did anything, except what Mum wanted. He's useless. Maybe your dad's different. Wow! Look!' She held up the photograph and, before their eyes, colour flowed back into each scratch like blue water into dry white river beds until there was no mark left; and what was equally strange was that the street scene in the background began to blur and shift, and they suddenly realized they were seeing a living picture.

'Cairo!' breathed Abe. It had to be, those figures, their clothes, the flowing robes, a woman in a chador. And his dad, looking directly at them: a thoughtful face, a strong face that made Abe think of an eagle: hooded eyes, a thin, curved nose, a thick black moustache, and a faint crease running up from the corner of his mouth as if a smile was just about to begin; and then, as they watched, he turned and walked away and within seconds had melted into the crowd. 'He's gone!' Abe turned the picture over as if somehow there would be his father still.

'What's it mean?'

'Wicked!'

'What?'

'Wicked, Nasfali. He's gone. He's free.'

'Flaming pharaohs!' breathed Abe. 'Thank you, Alicia Dunne. You have saved him.'

She gave him a funny look. 'It wasn't just me, Nasfali.'

But Abe wasn't listening. 'Do you think he saw us? That look at the end, do you think it was at us?'

'I don't know.' They sat in silence for a moment. 'I can see you've got to go, Nasfali. You have to find him. Take the papers from your box to the embassy, see if they can trace your family name. If we win, tomorrow, you'll have money for the air fare, and we'll have a bit in the pot to get us started.'

'Started for what? We must all go to Cairo!' exclaimed Abe. 'What will you do with the team? You can't stay here! Come with me, please. We'll find my father, and he'll help. The team will make us money, I know they will somehow. Listen, Alicia, we shouldn't even stay to play the match tomorrow. I don't even think they should play tomorrow. It's too risky.'

'I don't know. Even when you find your dad, how's he going to help, Nasfali? Think about it. Your mother was stronger than him, wasn't she? She had him trapped, not the other way round. And do you think the boys could stand the heat? It would finish them, the first match they play out there they'll get heart attacks. Is that what you want?'

'No.' Of course he didn't want that. 'I'll think of something.'

'Good. You think of something, Nasfali, I'm tired.'

Abe didn't want to let it go. 'But you can't stay here.'

'Oh? Bob said he reckoned he could help. He said the team would go a bomb in the States. All the senior citizens would love them. They could travel around in one of those silver airstreams, following the sun, playing football. I could drive.' She closed her eyes. 'It's Plan B, Nasfali.'

'You cannot be serious.'

'Why not. Mother would never follow me to America.'

'Of course she would . . . ' But Alicia was asleep, her head tilted sideways, and a peaceful smile on her face. She looked a different person, softer. The team would do what she said, he didn't doubt that, but it would be wrong for them to split up. They worked together. He felt safer with her. He wished she felt the same way. He switched off the overhead light. Plan B. Why had he not thought of a Plan B?

That night he dreamed of giant beefburgers the size of houses with the team bouncing up and down on the top, as if the huge buns were springy mattresses.

He woke with a start, the photograph, which was now just of a crowd of people in a busy street, clutched tightly in his hand. Five o'clock. The embassy yard was silent; the day thinly grey. He got up, eased past the sleeping Alicia and as quietly as he could, got down out of the bus. He took a deep breath, rubbed his face, and went over his late-night conversation with Alicia. America! America in a coach! Where was the poetry in that? Where was the glory?

He thought for a moment.

And where was the profit?

He walked up and down the outside of the bus. Stopped. Sniffed. And then scowled. The air smelt sour and cold and it made him think of his mother. And then of Mrs Dunne. He clenched his hands together. Where were they? Not far. Not far. Waiting to close in.

Of course Alicia and the team had to come with him but she thought the Egyptian heat would kill them. Would it? No, not if they stayed in the best hotel. The very best hotel! Of course! He could see it! It would be perfect: an entrance hall to marvel at with tall white pillars and cool marble floors; a pool edged in white stone and little fountains so all you would hear would be the sound of water, and maybe the gentle hum of a fan whirring overhead. Yes!

Then he pulled a face. How could they afford such a place, even when they had won their match?

He slapped his forehead. Guests of the country, that was how! Plan B. He, Ebrahim Nasfahl Ma'halli would see the ambassador and he would unfold his great scheme: the great match, the pyramids, and his team would be heroes, his team would be champions of the world. Guests of the country. Of course. All he had to do was convince the ambassador and that would surely be simple. He would wake Alicia and tell her, and she would tell the team. They would do what she wanted because they always did, and all would be well.

But it wasn't.

'Of course you can talk to them,' she said briskly, 'but I think my plan is best. What's the matter with you, Nasfali? You look weird.'

'No. Nothing.' She had suddenly reminded him of her mother. But that was not possible—she couldn't ever be like her, could she? But all that certainty he had felt such a little time before had gone and then, less than an hour and a half later, it looked as if it was all over. The team had risen, been fed and watered and were back in their places listening to him tell them of his great scheme, his Plan B. They liked it. They liked the idea of the great match but something was wrong. They were being too polite. 'Well,' he said, 'what do you think?'

None of them were even looking at him; they were looking at her. He looked at her too. And she shook her head.

'No.'

'Why not?'

'America will be safer,' she said, 'and America will be fun. Won't it, boys?'

And suddenly there were cheers, and the team looked happier.

'I don't mind going to America.' This was Jonson. 'Lots of films and we can go to a ranch.'

'Yee-ha!' yelled Jack. 'Giddy-up, Jonno.'

Laughter.

'You're wrong,' said Abe to Alicia. 'You really are.' She might be wonderful but she was being stubborn and stupid. 'My father will be there to help us.'

'Fathers!' And she shouted out to the team: 'Who needs fathers?'

'Not us!' they shouted back.

Abe ignored this. 'But you saw him,' he said to her. 'You know he's real.'

'I saw him disappearing, Nasfali. So did you. I'm sorry but I don't need your father. Independence is the thing, Nasfali, and anyway our trip to the States is sorted, I told you, while yours isn't. I'm doing what's best for the team, and what's best for me.'

'Are you?'

'Of course. Are they really going to let you see the ambassador? Be real.'

'Of course,' said Abe stiffly.

'Well, good for you.' She sniffed. 'You're the lucky one, Nasfali, you can go home; we can't.'

'But you can come with me!' She was exasperating. 'If you don't, your mother will get you.'

'No, she won't.'

He saw Bob walking from the main building towards their coach. 'I have to go. You stay if you must but think of the team. Maybe she won't do anything to you, but think what she'll do to them.' He didn't wait for an answer but hurried down the coach, making his goodbyes and trying to hide his fear. 'You'll be fine. You'll be splendid.' His heart felt like cold porridge. He shook their hands and, one by one, they tried to persuade him to stay with them.

'But you're the one who got us out,' said Jonson, who was sitting right at the back. 'You can't leave us now.'

But he had to. If he stayed, they would all be lost, he was sure of it. The only hope was to try his Plan B whether they wanted to come with him or not, because Alicia was wrong.

'Goodbye, Nasfali,' she said as he came back up the aisle. But he didn't get a chance to say anything because at that moment the door slid open and Bob poked his head into the bus. 'You guys ready to warm up because my boys are ready to rock and roll?'

Abe pushed past him and walked quickly to the gates where, without a word, the guard lifted the barrier for him, pressed a button, and the electronic gates swung silently open.

From the coach, Bob caught a last glimpse of the team's prickly schoolkid manager. 'What's eating that guy?' he said.

'He's going home,' said Alicia.

FIFTEEN

'It is out of the question. Who do you think you are, coming in here and making demands. You are a boy. Where is your mother? Where is your father? Go away. Go! I am busy.' The thin-faced official didn't even look up from the magazine which he was pretending was an important document. He merely snapped his long thin fingers, and then when he sensed that the boy hadn't disappeared, airily waved his hand as if to rid the air of a persistent fly.

Ebrahim Nasfahl Ma'halli—known to his friends as Abe or Nasfali—remained standing before the official's desk. He was quite calm and absolutely determined. He had walked through the early morning streets straight to the Egyptian embassy, arriving as the doors were being opened. He had ignored the frown of the London policeman on duty outside; he had ignored the uniformed door porter who had tried to tell him he could only come in with an adult; and now he ignored the flapping hand of the thin-faced, deskbound official. He had papers in his hand that proved he was indeed Ebrahim Nasfahl Ma'halli, and that his father was an Egyptian citizen, and so he, Ebrahim Nasfahl Ma'halli, had every right to the assistance of the Egyptian embassy. He had every right to see the ambassador himself. 'I have papers,' he said firmly. 'You will look at them, please.'

Taken slightly by surprise, perhaps, by the unexpected note of authority in the boy, the official looked up, discreetly shuffling a pile of papers on top of his copy of *Shoot*.

Though not yet busy, the reception hall, with its bank of desks manned by yawning officials, was beginning to fill. Queues formed, phones rang, and voices murmured.

The boy nodded. 'Man. United,' he said.

'What?'

'You support Manchester United. The magazine,' said the boy, lowering his voice slightly, 'I saw what you were reading. Not a bad team, though I manage a better one.'

The official swallowed and angrily stamped one of the documents he had in front of him. 'Nonsense. Boys do not manage football teams.'

'I do.'

An official at the neighbouring desk looked their way.

'What do you want?'

'First, I wish to see the ambassador.'

'Quite out of the question.'

'Second, I would like assistance in tracing my father . . . '

'That is also out of the question. You are a minor, of course, and, of course, a minor must have a parent to authorize such a request.'

'I am looking for my parent,' said Abe patiently.

'Where is your mother?'

'I don't know.'

'Then find her, bring her with you, and we will look into your request.' Satisfied that he had settled the matter, the official waved his hand again, stamped his stamp again, pursed his lips, and scratched something official on to the sheet in front of him.

Abe straightened his shoulders and concentrated. The official looked up and blinked. 'The reason I do not have a parent with me is because my mother has abandoned me, and I need your help to find my father.'

'Egypt,' said the official leaning forward across the desk and hissing at this extraordinarily persistent boy, 'does not need any more abandoned children.'

Abe raised his voice. 'Are you saying, that though I have these papers,' and he too leaned forward, and looked directly into the man's eyes, 'you will not help me?'

There was angry muttering from the people waiting in line behind him.

Abe was not deterred. 'Are you saying,' he repeated, more quietly this time, 'that Egypt does not care for children? I think you should allow me to see the ambassador.'

Abe was aware of someone jostling up beside him. 'Why do you not help the boy?' It was an elderly man, a string of prayer beads dangling from his knotty hand. 'What is it with you people?'

The official didn't appear to hear him. He merely shook his head, as if to clear it, and sat back in his chair. He pressed a buzzer on the corner of his desk and a light came on above them. 'Wait to one side,' he said to Abe. 'Someone will come to see to you.'

Abe turned to thank the elderly man but he was no longer there. Then he glimpsed him passing through a set of double doors at the inner end of the hall. Puzzled, he turned back to the official. The man had seemed familiar but he couldn't think why.

'What team?'

'What?'

'What is your team?'

'Oh, we played in the park,' said Abe, 'yesterday, against the Brazilian embassy team. We're training.'

'Oh,' said the official, slowly nodding his head, 'oh, that team. Oh yes. They are your team? You, a scruffy boy, have a team of old men, is that right.' Down came the stamp with an angry smack. 'What is this world! Next!'

At the same moment, a very smartly dressed young woman came up to him and told him to follow her and he did, through the same double doors as the old man had gone through.

'In here, please,' said the woman opening a door and ushering him into a thickly carpeted, simply furnished room: a long polished table stretched down towards floor-to-ceiling windows through which the sun poured. Two men stood by the window talking quietly to each other, but they turned when Abe was shown in.

'Ah,' said a familiar voice, 'the young man from the park. How interesting. Please,' and he beckoned Abe to come forward.

His eyes adjusting to the light, Abe recognized the elderly man from the downstairs hall. What was he doing here? He looked just like an ordinary, respectable, rather pious citizen. What was he doing in this posh room?

'Give me those papers you were waving around so much downstairs,' he said.

Abe did so.

'Thank you. Ma'halli,' he said, 'Ma'halli. I know, I know this name. Dalou, take this, please, run it through our computer. Find him.'

'Of course, your excellency.' And the second man took Abe's papers and discreetly left the room.

Your excellency? Abe stood up straight, and ran his hand through his hair. 'Are you the ambassador?'

'Mm.' The ambassador nodded. 'Yes, I am. Indeed I am, and you, strange boy, come into my embassy and start to tell my poor official what to do, as if this were your home and he your servant.'

'He was reading a football magazine.'

'Ah?' The ambassador raised one silvery eyebrow. 'Is this such a terrible crime?'

'No, but he should help me,' said Abe stubbornly. 'People like him always want to wave children away. They never listen.'

'When you go to Cairo, you too will wave children away,' said the ambassador.

'No,' said Abe. 'I won't.'

The ambassador studied him and then smiled, rather sadly, Abe thought. 'We have so many children in Egypt, why should we want one more?' His right thumb clicking the loop of prayer beads, one after another, after another. How many prayers would that be in a day, a week, a lifetime? 'Egypt has much trouble, so many people, all who want something. Did you know,' he continued, 'the

Nile runs a little thinner every day, and yet the sea creeps in all the time, threading salt into the soil. Why don't you stay here, strange boy, in this country? There would be many, many people, many children in Cairo who would swap with you.'

'No they wouldn't,' said Abe. 'There's nothing here . . . '

'Tsk!' The ambassador shook his head. 'No, no. There is football. There is the great Manchester United. Everybody wants to come to Britain for the football. You have a football team, strange boy. What else can you want? Do you know that all my embassy staff want to do is to play football. They play the other embassies, and they always lose. They lose to the Brazilians. They lose to the Americans. They are not happy. No, but then they see this strange thing. They see this team of old men beating Brazil, and they are even more depressed because they think, we are not old and still we lose. And then I find that a boy, who says he is Egyptian, manages this team but instead of doing great things with this team, he leaves them. He comes to me and says he wants to go to Cairo.'

'Yes.'

'That's it. I have no need to help you. If you have money you buy a ticket. If you don't then you stay here. It is simple.'

Abe looked down. 'I have no money. Not at the moment.'

'I thought as much,' said the ambassador. 'No money. And no parents. In Cairo, I am sorry to say, this is not so unusual, but you have more to tell me, I think, is that not so?'

Of course he had more to tell. This was the moment to unfold Plan B. This man was at the match in the park; he loved the team. Perhaps he would also love his great scheme. There was only one way to find out. He looked up and with what he hoped was his most businesslike manner he said: 'Yes, there is more.'

'I thought as much,' said the ambassador. 'Here, sit, have one of these and tell me your story and then we shall see what we shall see.' He pushed a white bowl with sugared fruits across the glass-topped table towards Abe.

Abe took one of the fruits. 'I had a great plan,' said Abe. 'It was a beautiful plan and I was coming here to give it to you when certain things happened which I shall explain in a moment.'

'Of course,' nodded the ambassador.

At that moment the door opened and the young assistant Dalou entered. 'I have the information you requested, your excellency.'

'Good, good. Give it to me and then sit here beside me and listen.'

The young assistant sat and handed over a single sheet of paper. The ambassador placed it on the table in front of him, but didn't even glance at it. 'Continue,' he said to Abe. 'I wish to hear your plan.'

'This plan was to bring my team to Cairo and there we would hold a world football championship for senior citizens. And all the matches would be held at Giza.'

'Yes, yes,' said the ambassador, 'I too have thought that this would be a fine place to have a football match. Go on, go on.'

And so Abe continued, and he painted the scene he had imagined so many times: the full moon, the great crowds, the dark mystery of the great pyramid presiding over everything. 'And, your excellency, the most fantastic thing for our country,' said Abe, 'is that there would be thousands of tourists flooding into the country because of the championship. We would have the Italians and the Chinese and the French . . . '

'And the Brazilians.'

'Of course, the Brazilians,' said Abe.

And the ambassador gave a gleeful laugh. 'And they will not win because your team will win everything. What do you think, Dalou? Get the minister for sport on the phone. E-mail the minister for tourism. E-mail everybody you can think of. This is marvellous. We will have this great championship.'

'Of course, your excellency, but there is one thing.' The young man leaned over and spoke quietly in the older man's ear.

'I see. I see. But this is just a detail, Dalou, do not be so petty. This young man here is Egyptian. Of course he is. His team is not but we, Dalou, are in the world of international sport. Everybody,' and he waved his hand excitedly round in the air, so that the loop of beads nearly clipped the young assistant on the nose, 'everybody changes countries and plays for other countries . . . apart from the Brazilians who think they are so marvellous.'

'Yes, your excellency.'

'Now, Dalou, now. I want a host of messages flying through the ether, Dalou, you see. I want the president himself to realize that we have produced this wonderful scheme. Does he like football, Dalou?'

'Who, your excellency?'

'The president, of course, the president.'

'I believe so, your excellency.'

'There is one thing,' said Abe, 'that I think you should . . . '

'Not now, strange boy, not now. Dalou, off you go. Good.'

After the young man had left the room, the ambassador turned to Abe. 'Now, what is it?'

'There is a problem,' said Abe.

'Of course, there is a problem, but,' he said pointing a bony finger at Abe, 'all problems can be solved. This is a lesson I have learned. With the help of God, and a little cunning, of course. What is this problem?'

'My team haven't exactly agreed to go to Cairo.'

'What! Where are they?'

Abe explained that they were at that moment playing the Americans in their embassy for a large sum of money.

The ambassador smiled and rubbed his hands when he heard this, admitting instantly to Abe that after his god, his country, and football, he loved betting more than everything. However, when Abe admitted that it was more complicated than this, that the team were in fact thinking of going to the United States, the ambassador snapped his fingers angrily.

'Old men are fools! What do they know? What do they know?'

'But it is worse still, your excellency,' said Abe, wondering quite how much of the truth he should reveal, 'they are being hunted. There are these women chasing them.'

'Ah,' said the ambassador, 'of course. It is their wives. You just go and convince them. That is what you must do. You say that we must have this championship. Say that they will fly first class to Cairo, that they will stay in the best hotel; that they can have burger and chip in Cairo and they can be in the land of the pharaohs at the same time. Tell them that, strange boy.' He picked up the paper that his assistant had brought in to him and read it quietly. Then he nodded and put it back on the glass table. 'As I thought, your family name is indeed familiar to me.'

'You have traced my father?'

'Not exactly, but we know who he is . . . or was.'

'Was? He is alive. I know he is,' said Abe.

'Hm. But you know nothing else about him? Not who he was or what he did? Nothing? Is that right?'

'My mother refused to speak of him.'

'I can understand,' said the ambassador, nodding. 'She regretted her marriage and came back to her home country.'

'Yes. She regretted marrying him.'

'It is not a surprise. Your father, I am sorry to say, is a convicted criminal. A clever man, it says here, a talented man. Thirteen years in prison.'

Abe felt his cheeks grow hot. His mother a witch and

his father, his father whom he thought, whom he hoped would welcome him into a new life, turned out to be a criminal. It wasn't fair. Who else had a life like this? All those boys at school with ordinary families, why couldn't he have an ordinary life, an ordinary family? And then he thought of the team. Life hadn't been fair to them, either. Worse, in fact. And Alicia. Imagine having Mrs Dunne for your mother. No, maybe life was just odd and you had to put up with it.

'What did he do?' he asked resignedly.

'He was a forger. Money, I suppose. No, wait, something about national treasures, trying to smuggle things out of the country. He was released . . . yesterday. Strange, no?'

Oh yes, very strange: a box hidden away in his mother's den. A box with no hinge that could only be opened when he and Alicia had concentrated together. Abe frowned. That had been a kind of magic but it must have come from Alicia, not him.

And in the box, an old photograph of his father, his smiling face scratched out. The box and photograph had all been part of his mother's power in keeping his father locked away. Basic bad magic, Alicia had called it. Take the photograph from the box, thought Abe, and the real prison doors swing open.

She must have really hated him, but then it didn't take much to make a witch hate. Still, he wondered what it was that his father had done. Maybe like Abe he had tried to take something from her, or maybe she had wanted something from him. There was only one way to find out. 'Is there an address?'

'No, no more records. I am sorry. It seems we are both to be disappointed. What will you do?'

'Find him,' said Abe. 'I shall go to Cairo. All I need is a passport. If the team wins, they will give me my share, it will be enough for a ticket.'

'Good. Perhaps you would like to phone them, see

how they are doing. Persuade them to change their minds.' He pushed the phone down the glass table towards Abe. 'Press that button there and just ask. They will put you through.'

Should he? What if they were losing? What if Mrs Dunne had found them? What then? 'I don't know,' he said. 'Perhaps I should wait.' He stared at the phone, aware that the ambassador was watching him. 'When I get to Cairo, where should I look? Where should I begin?'

'The city of the dead, perhaps,' said the ambassador drily.

And then, at that moment, the phone rang, a discreet double ring, so soft that Abe thought that perhaps he had imagined it. And then, it rang again. The ambassador reached out and took the phone. He listened for a moment and then passed it to Abe. 'For you,' he said softly. 'The phone is for you, strange boy, strange Ma'halli.'

Sixteen

T he voice at the end of the phone was very quiet, as if she didn't want to be overheard. 'I want to speak to Ebrahim Nasfali, is he there? Hello? I was asking . . . '

'Alicia, what's the matter? What is it?'

'Nasfali. Oh, Nasfali, I made a mistake.' She paused. He heard something that sounded like crying in the background and then her voice again, but uncertain as if she were no longer sure whom it was that she was talking to. 'Nasfali? Is that you?'

'Yes.'

'Can you get us out of here?'

'What do you mean?' He looked up, aware that the old, keen-eyed ambassador was watching him closely. At the other end of the line he could now hear crackling and hissing and then a sudden sharp intake of breath. 'Alicia, what is it? Are you all right?'

'I can't . . . Nasfali, she is stronger than I am. She's making the boys see things and I can't stop her. And I don't want to be like her. I don't. You have to hurry, Nasfali. It's your turn.'

He felt a chill down his neck and saw, once again, that awful underground wasteland into which his mother had somehow cast him. Is that what had happened to her? He gripped the phone: 'Where are you?'

'Here.' And then, 'They're coming.'

There was a click and Abe found himself staring through the glass of the table down to the scuffed toes of his trainers and the polished wooden floor and listening to the buzz of the dead phone. The witches had found Alicia and the team, that's what had happened.

The ambassador cleared his throat. 'The girl?'

'Yes.' He replaced the phone. 'She's gone,' he said. How could he help her? She was the one who seemed to be able to do things; except, said a small voice at the back of his head, you were the one who released the team from the photograph. But he hadn't; he had just been standing there. No, persisted the small voice, you were the one.

'Where has she gone?' The ambassador's thumb paused its endless clicking of the beads. 'Has the team gone with her?'

'No. No, I meant that she was cut off, that's all. She wants me to get her from the embassy.'

'Is this so terrible?'

How could he explain? Well, you see, your excellency, my friend's mother is a witch . . . No, he couldn't begin to tell the truth but he had to move fast. It didn't sound as if Alicia could hold out long. He cleared his throat. 'I don't think they will let her or the team go. She didn't say why.' He pulled a face. 'Perhaps it was to do with documents or passes . . . and the women I mentioned, the ones chasing them . . . '

'Ah! Their wives and papers, documents, of course. But this is nothing. We shall manage. These Americans love paper but more, more they love to win at everything. This team, they will want to keep them. They won their match, yes, your team, they won?'

'She didn't say.'

'Of course, and now they must come here where they will be safe.' He clapped his hands together and his thin face split into a delighted smile. 'We shall make a visit, a diplomatic visit and there will be a little diplomatic incident,' and he winked at Abe, who wasn't sure whether he was supposed to wink back because he had no idea what the ambassador had in mind, so he merely nodded.

The ambassador stood up. 'We must hurry,' he said and taking up the phone, he impatiently jabbed at the numbers on the front. 'Ah, Dalou, good . . . ' and he spoke rapidly in Arabic. Then he put the phone down.

'And she is being kept there against her will. You are sure of this?'

'She wouldn't ring otherwise. What is your plan, your excellency.'

'Oh, a message has been sent to my dear friend the American ambassador saying that I shall be coming over immediately, unofficially of course, so no red tape, no American papers necessary. I shall be coming in my cars.' Abe wondered how many cars he usually travelled in. 'And I shall want to meet this team that I watched in the park. It is simple. They will see my cars. They will open the gates. We shall drive in. There will be your girl and the football team. They will get in and we shall drive out. Who can stop us?'

A miracle! A gift from Egypt to him. 'We shall fly in like desert hawks, your excellency,' Abe said. 'But how will everyone fit in the cars?'

'You will see. Very big cars. And then when they are all here, we will tell them that they will be very happy in Cairo, and they will say yes. And there we are. Do you never smile, strange boy?'

Abe smiled.

When Abe and the ambassador came out of the double doors at the rear of the embassy there were two huge, black stretch limousines with darkened glass windows, and a tiny Egyptian pennant on the bonnet of each. Beside each car was a uniformed driver. 'There you are,' said the ambassador. 'You go in that one. They will take you there. Talk to no one but your friends. Be quick when you are there. The Americans will not be happy, but then,' he said with a shrug, 'one cannot always be happy. The drivers are instructed.'

'You're not coming?'

'No. It would not be so good. Discretion, strange boy Ma'halli. Discretion. That is the gift of age. Now go.'

Abe wasn't sure what the ambassador meant but he got into the leading car anyway and found himself lurching face down into the soft upholstery of the back seat as the driver roared the limousine out of the embassy and on to the main road.

Abe watched intently, first from one window and then the other. He peered at cars that pulled up alongside them, he stared at pedestrians at traffic lights waiting to cross, at shoppers clustered round windows. Where were they? Where were Mrs Dunne and her followers?

The driver held up one finger and his thickly accented voice came through the little speaker by the window: 'American embassy one minute.' Then Abe saw the grey gates and the driver pulled up outside. He gave a long blast on the horn and they swung open. The duty marine stepped over to the driver's window. The driver flipped open a wallet and the guard stepped back and saluted in Abe's direction, the white gauntlet snapping up and down like a railway signal. Abe shrank back into his seat and then relaxed. Tinted windows, of course, no one could see in.

They pulled away, slowly this time. Abe looked behind. The other limousine was following. He glanced along the wall. Bare. How easy would it be for the witches to enter one of these high security buildings? It depended on how powerful they were, he supposed. How ready they were to make themselves visible to the world.

He saw the pitch and the coach. There were two guards and an official from the embassy standing beside it, talking. Then over by the steps of the main building, he saw the team, all gathered round Alicia.

The limousine pulled up beside them. Abe lowered the window. 'Come on,' he called, 'get in, quick!'

They stared at him blankly. Alicia had her arms round two of them—skinny Bittern and round Roberts. What was happening?

Abe's driver got out and stepped towards them, and

they all shrank back, including Alicia, as if he were some monster. The driver turned and shrugged at Abe. 'What is this? I am told they are to come with us.'

'I know.' Abe glanced back at the coach; the three men were still there. He swung open the door of the limo and walked up to them. Twelve pairs of eyes followed his every move. 'What is it? What's the matter?'

Alicia pulled a face and shuddered slightly. 'Is it you, Nasfali?'

'Of course it's me. You told me to come and get you. I came. I'm here. Come on.' He looked at the team. Half of them were in tears, the rest of them were white-faced and drawn. They were still in their games kit and they looked scuffed and muddy and battered. Griffin was holding his arm awkwardly. 'What's the matter with everyone? Alicia, what is it?'

She shook her head. 'I don't know. My mother is very close. Perhaps just outside. Did you see her?' He shook his head. 'And the Americans have changed. They seem suspicious. And they were rough. The game was bad, Nasfali. It's her, changing everything.'

'I can see my dad,' whimpered Roberts. 'He's over there. Why won't he come and get me? He's over there.'

'What! What's he talking about? Alicia, wake up! Let's go.' Through the glass entrance doors, he could see the once friendly Bob, talking to two marines. Abe knew exactly what would happen next so he grabbed Bittern and Jonson and hustled them towards the limousine. 'Get in. Now. All of you.' He turned back to Alicia. 'Come on,' he shouted. 'Hurry! It's the park all over again. Look at the guards.' They seemed bigger, fatter; their faces bloated and sweaty behind dark glasses that now seemed absurdly small. Lakins in uniform, and all of them staring their way.

Alicia suddenly seemed to wake up. 'Yes. Into the cars, quickly.' She guided Roberts who stumbled down the two steps and seemed to falter, reluctant to get in the car. 'No, get in. It's not your father.'

'Are you sure?'

'Yes.'

Abe pushed the last two into the second car and then jumped in beside Alicia in the first car. The driver turned and raised his thumb. Abe nodded. The good old thumbs up. And they were off. Just in time too, as the doors burst open and Bob and the marines came running down towards them.

'Halt!' shouted one of the guards.

'Down,' shouted Abe. Everyone in their car shrank forward, but there was no crack, no splinter of glass, nor lurching squeal as a tyre was hit. Abe lifted his head. The barrier was down and the electronic gates were slowly swinging shut. He banged on the glass. 'Don't stop!' he yelled. 'Don't stop.'

'No problem for number one car!' shouted the driver, his voice booming out of the speaker, as they accelerated towards the blocked exit. The marine who had saluted them in stood by the barrier and then began to back away uncertainly, raising his gun as he did so.

This time there was a crack, in fact two, one immediately after the other. The first caused a tiny star shape to bloom in the side window where the guard's bullet struck and the other, louder crack was the splintering of the barrier as they smacked it aside, and then another grinding squeal as they plunged into the narrowing gap of the closing gates, and the metal edge scoured along the flank of the limousine but they forced their way through, the car behind jolting out after them.

'Yes!' shouted Abe. 'We've done it.'

Alicia opened her eyes. 'Yes,' she said, 'and there's mother.'

Abe twisted about and saw her standing with a group of women dressed in sharp suits, on the pavement opposite the entrance to the embassy, staring hard at the limos.

'I knew it,' she said. 'I knew they were very near.'

'We're all right now, though. I got you out. It was

152

my turn, Alicia, and I rescued you.' He couldn't help puffing himself up. It was good. He had been, after all, something of a hero. 'We are equals.'

'Yes,' she said, 'you were wicked, but it's getting harder. I don't know how long we can keep ahead of them.'

'We don't have far to go, and I have it arranged. That's if you agree. We can leave our mothers behind for good.'

'Egypt?' Alicia smiled, nodded, and closed her eyes.

They moved down through the traffic, cars swerving to give their battered limousine a wide berth, and then just as the embassy dropped out of sight, Abe caught the driver's eyes in the mirror and they were cold and winter grey. Abe shuddered and blinked and then the driver was looking back over his shoulder, grinning at him and giving him the good old thumbs up. But for a split second, it hadn't been the driver, the Egyptian embassy driver, he had seen in the mirror, but his mother, and her lips had moved, mouthing a single word: 'Stay.'

Their power was growing.

SEVENTEEN

'Oh!'

The sky had darkened into a dirty dishrag and rain was beginning to spatter off the dented, black limousines. London in July had scrumpled itself into a sullen and wintry mood.

'Is this truly my car?'

'I am sorry, your excellency,' said Abe, frowning, 'they tried to close the gates on us. It wasn't your driver's fault.' He spoke automatically, apologetically, politely. He had introduced Alicia, he had introduced the team who looked as battered and worn as the once shiny car, and now he stood beside the ambassador, waiting to hear whether or not he would be willing to help them further.

'It is nothing,' the ambassador suddenly decided. 'What are cars, strange boy, mere pieces of metal to take us from here to there.' He clicked his fingers contemptuously in the air and then patted Abe on the shoulder. 'Come in. Come in. We must find accommodation for your dear friends. We must find them sustenance. We must prepare them for their journey. We do not worry about the cars; you will pay me back tenfold, when you are rich, strange boy, when you are rich. Do not look so concerned.'

In fact Abe was barely listening. His mind kept returning to the disturbing image of his mother's eyes and her lips saying 'Stay'. Why? She had never wanted him. No, just the box with the photograph. Well, she was too late.

'Here,' said the ambassador. 'This is a fine room. You will be comfortable in here.' He looked back at the glum group of elderly men still in their muddy shorts, who were standing around Alicia as she knelt on the floor, tending to Jonson. 'I will arrange for you to have baths, and food will be brought, yes.'

Alicia stood and came over to Abe and the ambassador. 'I don't know what is the matter,' she said. 'He collapsed halfway through the match. I think he needs a doctor.'

'The match you won, of course.'

'Yes.'

'He is probably just tired,' said Abe. 'Let him rest.' He made a face at Alicia that the ambassador couldn't see. If it looked as if the team weren't well enough to play again, then what chance of them being flown to Egypt?

'Are you sure.' She gave him an intent look. 'All right. We'll see how he gets on.' She bit her lip. 'I expect you want to know whether they paid up the winnings?' she said to Abe.

'Winnings,' exclaimed the ambassador. 'Isn't that a beautiful word? We shall have many winnings when you arrive safely in Cairo.'

'What?' said Alicia. 'Nasfali, have you agreed something without telling me?'

'It is just a possibility. Plan B, you know,' said Abe, trying to work out from Alicia's expression whether they really had won the money. 'Your excellency, would you explain what you have arranged for us all.'

'No, no, you tell them, they are your team, strange boy.' He lowered his voice so only Abe could hear: 'I have seats for two o'clock tomorrow morning. All of you. Here are all the necessary documents.' He slipped a brown envelope into Abe's hand. 'It is settled. You will be met at Cairo airport and taken to a hotel. No, no, don't thank me. It is a marvellous plan. And you will have to work hard when you are there, strange boy, you will have to help set up this championship. Many meetings. Very many.' He raised his voice again. 'I have business now. Did you know,' he said, turning back in the doorway, a sly smile on his face, 'that our American friends have had trouble with the police.'

'I saw there were a couple of policemen,' said Abe.

'Yes. Apparently, a stolen bus or coach was discovered

there. The police are investigating, but it seems my dear friend the American ambassador could be charged with being in possession of stolen property.' One hooded eye closed in a hawk-like wink. 'Isn't that a terrible thing?'

'He seems all right,' said Alicia. She sat down and crossed her legs, hitching her short dress down towards her knees. She looked as wild and scrumpled as the team, grass stains on her dress and mud on her boots. But she did not look happy.

'Yes,' said Abe, 'I like him. And my great scheme, Alicia, for the championship held in front of the Great Pyramid of Giza, he loves it and he'll help make it happen . . . '

'Is that what we all want?'

'Do you have another plan?'

'No,' she sighed. 'It's just that I know what you want, Nasfali. You have a plan, your plan, for yourself, but does it really take into account them,' she gestured at the scattered team.

At that moment Jonson gave a moan and Thomas who was looking after his friend called out: 'Miss Dunne!'

She gave Abe a look as if to say 'you see what I mean' and hurried over to him.

He watched her. Then he looked around at the other members of the team sitting in sad lumpy knots of one or two, not talking, not doing anything. Of course, he was thinking of them as well as himself and her. They would be safe there; they would have a chance to be famous and, and . . . He struggled to think into the future and what next year or the year after would hold for Griffin and Pike and the others. It was something for them, wasn't it? If they were famous, they would make money and would be able to have somewhere to live. It was all possible because he had made friends with the ambassador and he had liked his scheme. Didn't she see that? And if they had won the bet, then they were even better off.

He should have been feeling pleased too but he was distracted. There was a constant niggling, like little claws scratching at the edge of his thoughts: his mother. He didn't want to think about her but he couldn't help it. He could almost hear her voice. He felt that she was close. Involuntarily he turned round, half expecting to see her at his shoulder. No. Not yet.

Food was brought, and the team perked up a little. Clean clothes arrived too: plain shirts and an assortment of white cotton trousers. The team helped themselves, while Abe himself struggled to fight off his own growing sense of gloom.

'I hope they don't want us to play cricket,' said Jissop. 'I hate cricket. Tock. Tock. Stupid ball and a stupid bat.'

'I say, Jissop, stop being an old woman, there's a good chap.'

'We look like sailors.'

'You look like angels,' said Alicia.

'Old angels,' said Bittern sadly.

'Old fat angels,' said Griffin. 'And I have a rotten sprained wing.'

'Won't get to heaven then, will you?'

Alicia stood beside Abe. 'Talk to them,' she said. 'You're the manager. You haven't even congratulated them for winning this.' She dumped a fat brown doughnut bag on to his lap.

'The money!' He peered inside the bag. There it was! A delicious scrumped mess of ten and twenty pound notes. One thousand pounds! A hundred times more money than he'd ever made in all his schemes put together. He punched the air. 'Yes!'

She looked at him coolly. 'Is that all you care about?'

'No, of course not. But it's a prize; it's very good. What's the matter, Alicia? Don't you think it's good?'

'Money!' She sniffed. 'It doesn't interest me. Maybe it's more a boys' thing.'

'What is it? We got away from them, didn't we? Can't you see, Alicia, it's like a sign. Don't you feel it?'

'I don't know.' She rubbed her eyes, and touched the ring on her nose. She looked tired and she looked different too, as if she couldn't make her mind up about something. 'Tell them,' she said. 'It'll make them happy anyway.' She winced.

'Have you hurt yourself?'

She shook her head. 'It's mother. Don't mind me. You speak to the boys.'

He watched her as she moved away towards Jonson, then looked down at the money in his hands. They could do it! They would get away. No mothers were going to stop them, not even if they gathered all the witches of England and made them stand across the runway.

He jumped up on to a coffee table and stamped his foot to get the team's attention.

Heads turned immediately. Jack burped and Griffin crowed: 'Look at Jimmy jump. Jimmy's got jumpy.'

Roberts cuffed him. 'Don't call him that, he doesn't like it.'

'Listen everybody!'

They listened. They listened while he told them how great they were. He asked them who had scored the winning goal and when they said Roberts, he made them all give him three cheers and Roberts went pink with pleasure, and smiled down at his tummy. He told them that everything was fixed for them. He showed them the money.

'How much did we win?' called Jack.

'One thousand pounds!' He grabbed a fistful of notes and held them up for them to see.

They goggled and gaped. 'That's a lot of money,' said Thomas, his hand drifting up to stroke his bald head.

'Are we millionaires?' wondered Stokely.

'Not quite, but you could be,' said Abe.

He told them that there was a plane waiting for them on the runway at Heathrow Airport. That one of the best hotels in Cairo was booked for them. 'Are you ready to play the match of your lives?' he asked them. 'Are you ready for a world championship?'

They whooped.

They yelled.

They shouted.

They threw their dirty shorts in the air.

'Are you happy to come with me then?' He saw Alicia hurrying over to the window. 'My dad will be there to help us.'

As if they had been stung, the team suddenly fell silent. At the same moment that horrible scratching started again, little claws behind his eyes it seemed now. He took a deep breath to start again; the air tasted sour. He saw Alicia turning away from the window and looking at him, her face white with worry.

And then the storm came. He saw a spider flicker of white, forked lightning and then the rumble and crack of thunder directly overhead, so loud the building trembled.

'I don't want to go to Egypt.'

Stokely started to snivel. 'I want to go home.'

They all wanted to go home.

He tried to tell them that their homes had gone but none of them were listening. They were just like they had been when he rescued them from the American embassy: bewildered and lost.

'I saw my dad. We passed him on the way here.'

'I saw my mummy.'

'And mine.'

'And mine.'

They had all seen their mums, their dads, their brothers and sisters. Even though their mums and dads were long dead and their brothers and sisters scattered far and wide.

There were more tears and though Abe shouted, they wouldn't stop. The storm raged. Thunder rumbled. It became almost impossible to hear or to think. Abe began to feel anger building up in him. 'You can all go to—' he started to shout but then Alicia was at his side, shaking his arm.

'Don't say it. You don't mean it.' She tugged him towards the window.

'Let me go.'

He tried to shake her off but she wouldn't let go. It wasn't fair. Why had it all gone wrong? Why was she pointing at her watch.

Midnight.

She grabbed his shoulders and twisted him round, forcing him to look outside.

And there was the answer. Beyond his reflection, he saw the outer gate swinging open and figures filing into the yard. They moved swiftly, purposefully, ignoring the rain and the lightning. And then Abe could see that they were the women in dark suits; their hair was plastered to their heads, their faces pale. They moved into a smooth semicircle facing the building and their heads tilted, looking up. He felt their eyes boring into him.

The thunder rolled back into the distance.

This was why the mood in the room had changed. This was why Jonson was so ill, and all of them so miserable.

Abe felt Alicia's hand on his arm.

'What do we do?'

'Wait,' she said.

'I'm sorry,' said Abe. 'I wasn't really going to say anything bad.'

'I know.'

'It's them, isn't it? They can change people, can't they?'

'I'm not changed,' she said. 'Nor are you.'

'What happens now?'

'Don't you feel it?'

He did. It was as if a hand was gripping his elbow, and another gripped his chin, turning his head, another pressing on the small of his back. He began to walk, stumbling towards the door. 'Alicia!' He couldn't turn his head to see if she was being made to come too. 'Alicia!'

'I'm here.' She sounded very cross. 'We're all here. We're all together, Nasfali.'

'Are you angry, Alicia?' He felt his jaw clamping, his words squeezed through clenched teeth.

'I could spit fire,' she muttered.

Eighteen

The team came out of the embassy building, faltering, awkward, pulled inexorably by the power of the waiting witches. Down the steps and into the high-walled yard they came and as the cold wind swirled around them and the thin rain sliced down on them, they shuddered and clustered sheep-like around Alicia and Abe.

'Miss Dunne?'

'Miss Dunne, what's happening?'

'I think I've had a bad dream.'

'It's all right, boys.'

It wasn't, of course. Behind them the embassy building was silent and dark: no one manned the reception desk and no guards patrolled the long carpeted corridors. Beyond the walls of the embassy, for maybe half a mile or more, all the streets were silent and dark.

The witches stood on the far side of the yard, as still as stone statues, their hair plastered to their heads, their suits sodden. They stood stock still, yet as if ready to spring: hands half clenched, knees bent, leaning forward. They stood staring, their eyes black pits, and their faces smudged and smeared by the rain so they all looked horribly the same.

Abe felt Alicia's shoulder against his, the back of her hand against his. What should they do? What could they do? 'Alicia?' He was so frightened. All he could see were the sisters standing in a half circle, like the jaws of a trap. 'Alicia?' Her hand gripped his.

'Do you have a plan, Nasfali?'

He shook his head. 'Do you?'

'Concentrate.'

On what? Concentrate on what? She was the one. She

rescued him before. 'Alicia,' he said, his voice a bare murmur, 'you can do something. You have power. I know you have.'

No response. With a huge effort he turned his head to look at her. Her eyes were closed, her nostrils flared as she breathed in and out, heavily, and her lips 'tremoring' as if she were inwardly muttering some words or chant, over and over.

The team suddenly stirred and pressed close together. Alicia's eyes snapped open: green, cold, shards of ice. Her fingers clamped round Abe's hand so tightly that he felt the bones in his knuckle click. He winced and turned to see what Alicia was staring at with such fierce anger.

One of the witches had stepped forward and in a splash of lightning, Abe saw that it was Mrs Dunne, a red silk scarf knotted round her throat—her head thrown back, her fleshy nose tilted as if she were scenting them.

'Can't you do something now? Please, Alicia, before she does something terrible.'

No answer.

They couldn't stand there, and do nothing. He pushed the fear down, and unclenched Alicia's hand from his. He stepped forwards out into the open space.

'Leave us alone,' he shouted, somehow managing to control the quaver in his voice. 'Go back and leave us alone.'

Mrs Dunne sniffed and shuddered and suddenly there was a crackling, popping sound rising up behind Abe. A splintering and snapping like ice, or glass. He glanced back, and was astonished to see first one window crack into a thousand white lines, and then another and another, rippling up from the ground floor as far as he could see into the darkness.

Mrs Dunne did that?

He turned back. She had her arms out, reaching towards them, her fingers hooked into claws. 'Alicia.' Her voice seemed to come from everywhere. 'Alicia. Join us, Alicia.'

Abe scanned the faces of Mrs Dunne's dark company, looking for his mother. There. That one. Third on the right, not even looking at him but, like all the others, seeing only the girl. 'Leave her alone!' he shouted. 'She's not like you. She doesn't want to be like you, any of you. You can't do anything to change her or us, not unless . . . ' Unless what, what had he been going to say? Unless he or Alicia desired the kind of power the sisters had. He felt a black flood of despair because that was exactly what they wanted. Only if they had power could they defeat Mrs Dunne. But how could they get that power without becoming like one of the sisters? It was a trap.

'Had you been born a daughter, Nasfali,' hissed Mrs Dunne, 'your mother, my sister, might hear you. But you are . . . a mistake.'

He staggered back a step, buffeted off balance by the force of her venom.

'You're nothing to us. You're a worm. Your team are worms. All who do not belong with me are worms.'

Abe felt as if the words were pummelling him, making him stumble, forcing him backwards.

'So slither,' said Mrs Dunne, 'like a worm back to your dead friends.'

Suddenly Abe felt the ground being snatched away from his feet. He clattered, gasping, to the wet ground. His hands stung, his head thrummed and for a moment everything was out of focus. He twisted away from Mrs Dunne. He was useless, no help to Alicia at all; he couldn't even see her properly.

Then he heard Alicia's voice. 'They're not dead,' she snapped icily.

'They all died,' said Mrs Dunne. 'They were on a train and the train exploded. It was in the papers, my dear.'

'It was a lie. One of your lies!'

'Choose, Alicia. Become one of us, or join those worms when I stuff them back behind a frame, and hang them up for ever. Twelve there'll be with Nasfali. And if you make me,' she said thinly, 'you'll hang there too— number thirteen.'

'You don't know what you are doing. You don't know what you have done. One of them is sick. He is dying. No one can die twice.'

'Oh?' Mrs Dunne took another step forward, raised her right arm and pointed at the group of old boys. Jonson jerked suddenly and fell. 'I know what I have done now. He'll live, for the moment, and then if I put him back in the frame he can spend an eternity dying. It's up to you what happens. Come back, Alicia. You can't help yourself. Come back and I'll leave them alone.' From the darkness she conjured a black photo frame and held it up. 'Remember this, all of you.' The team stood transfixed, white-faced, trembling. 'We do not ever forgive, we don't ever forget.'

'Never forgive,' murmured the sisters.

The team groaned.

Alicia bowed her head.

Oh, Alicia, he prayed, as he lay still pinned to the ground, don't go back. There's no hope if you go back to her.

'I see,' said Mrs Dunne. 'I see.' She too was angry. The air, charged with electricity, flickered around her. Her voice shook. 'I see that you continue to challenge, Alicia, I see—'

She suddenly stopped short as one of the team broke away from the group, and stood panting in front of Alicia, shielding her with his large frame from her mother. It was Roberts, their stocky centre forward. It was Roberts, the one, Abe remembered, who had mistaken Alicia for her mother. It was Roberts who Mrs Dunne had had a passion for when she was just a little girl. It was Roberts who had teased her.

'I am so sorry,' he said. 'I've wanted to say this a hundred times. I really am sorry. I wish I could turn back the clock. I really do.' And before Mrs Dunne could react, he had darted forward and kissed her on the cheek.

The effect was extraordinary: Mrs Dunne spluttered. Her pink cheeks burned bright red; her mouth opened; the frame trembled in her hand and the glass snapped and shivered into shards on the ground. Something like a moan emerged from her mouth, and from the mouths of all the semicircle of sisters. Their heads tilted back, their mouths widened, the moan grew louder and louder and thinned into a piercing, terrifying howl. Lights and alarms suddenly exploded into life. Bulbs brightened and burst, the two limousines roared into life and one of them rocked forward and slammed straight into the wall, its bonnet snapping open like a mouth. Abe and the team reeled backwards, pressing their hands to their ears to try to block the sound that pinched their eardrums and made their eyes water with pain.

Only Alicia stood unmoved.

Abe scrambled forward. They wouldn't have her. He wouldn't let it happen. He was about to grip her arm to pull her back when he stopped. She was ghost white, her skin translucent, her hands raised, white and flickering. From the tips of her fingers streamed blue light that ripped across the dark, like sudden slashes of a knife, here, there, and where the light struck, it tore holes through metal and stone. The already damaged limo exploded, sending a tyre spinning up high into the air. The interior was a cauldron of orange flame. Abe hugged the ground.

The witches themselves seemed locked into their howl, unable to stop, unable to move as Alicia's wild magic scored around them. One of the sisters on the end of the semicircle was caught in the blue light and was hurled backwards, straight through a hole that had been torn in the night and suddenly she was gone.

Face pressed into the wet cold tarmacadam of the yard, Abe knew that this was their only chance. He twisted round and yelled at the team, all of whom like him were now spread-eagled on the ground. 'Get to the car!' he shrieked. 'That one. That one.' He grabbed Griffin and pointed. 'Get them there, now!'

Griffin was stunned but he understood. He grabbed Thomas who was beside him and between them they hauled Jonson to his feet and then the others, seeing what was happening, followed suit. Crouching as low as they could, they scuttled and ducked and weaved their way to the surviving limousine and shoved and pushed each other in through the door.

Abe stared at Alicia as the fire storm flailed from her fingers. Then he shut his eyes. Took a deep breath. Saw once again the image of his father, smiling and disappearing down that street somewhere in Cairo, imagined once again the great match in front of the pyramid at Giza, saw, once again, himself and Alicia dark figures on a high moonlit dune looking down to the green land of the Nile. Then he scrabbled himself up ready to spring and hurled himself in a low dive. He felt a searing pain across the top of his scalp, and smelt scorching, then he collided with Alicia's legs and brought her tumbling to the ground. Frantically he grabbed her arms and pinned them to her side, then hauled her to her feet.

The impact, the shock, seemed to have shaken her out of her mad fury. She seemed drained, helplessly weak. Abe had to half carry her, half drag her towards the car, expecting at any second to be snatched back by Mrs Dunne.

Suddenly the limo bucked and screeched into action ramming bits of smouldering wreck in front of it and lurching up to Abe. The passenger door was opened and Abe shoved Alicia in and then scrambled in beside her.

It was Griffin at the wheel. 'I think I have the hang of it now,' he shouted and the limo leapt forward, past the sisters, some of whom were on their knees, others stumbling forward, hands outstretched, trying to catch at the car, knowing or sensing their prey was escaping. But the limo surged on, through the gate and into the dark street.

'Where to, governor?' said Griffin.

'Heathrow,' said Abe.

'Where's that?'

'I've no idea.'

NINETEEN

The car was cold; the atmosphere tense and silent. Alicia was barely conscious. Abe held both her hands in his and rubbed them to warm them. He tried to ignore the way her head lolled against his shoulder. She was making little snorting noises through her ringed nose but at least she was alive, at least she was safe. But Abe was worried. He didn't know what all that fizzing power had done to her. He imagined it must have felt as if she'd swallowed a bolt of lightning. It must have been burning her up inside, burning her heart, burning her brain. He forced himself to think about the team.

'Is everyone safe?'

Griffin, peering through the smeary windscreen into the darkness, gave a non-committal grunt. He was concentrating like mad, his head poked forward so far that his skinny nose was practically touching the wheel. He looked like a tortoise stretching out of his shell.

Abe glanced at the speedometer: it registered a flickering twenty miles an hour. He hoped Mrs Dunne and her sisters didn't have anything faster than bicycles or they'd catch up with them in no time. He craned round and tried unsuccessfully to do a headcount; large as the limo was, they were still squashed together like beans in a tin. He found the switch which allowed the connecting speaker to work: 'Everyone all right?'

There were a couple of muted groans and one puzzled: 'I'm sitting on Gannet's armpit.' Then Griffin misjudged a corner and banged on to the kerb and a chorus of yelps and squeals emerged from the back. To Abe it sounded as if most of the team were there. 'Sorry, skipper,' Griffin muttered, 'nearly got the hang of it.'

Abe took a deep breath. The streets were black. Griffin

was doing his best but neither he nor Abe had any idea which way they should be going. He made Griffin stop, which he did with a ferocious jolt.

Abe slowly called out the team's names, and they all answered one after the other. When he came to Roberts there were a few jeers at 'lover boy' but the teasing was half hearted and it stopped when Abe pointed out that the only reason that they weren't at that moment squashed behind a glass frame was because of Roberts and Alicia.

Then Abe called out Jonson's name. No reply. 'Where's Jonson?' He felt a tightening panic. They couldn't go back; but they couldn't leave him either, could they? What harm had he ever done to anyone?

'He was with me and Griffin,' said Thomas. 'He must be here; we shoved him through the door.'

Then a faint and muffled voice said: 'It's all right, chaps, I'm here.'

Abe felt some of the tension ease. 'How do you feel?'

'All right, I think. I didn't feel very well at the embassy, skipper. I think I passed out.'

Alicia, wedged up against his shoulder, stirred. 'Nasfali,' she said, her voice faint but still imperious, 'why have we stopped?'

'Alicia, you're all right!' He wanted to tell her that she was more wonderful than the most powerful queen the world had ever seen. He wanted to tell her that when she raised her arms and poured blue fire into the night, she was both beautiful and terrible. No wonder her mother wanted her with them: she had more power than any of the sisters. Wild magic, no rules, no control; that would frighten them. Now that she was awake perhaps they would be safe, perhaps Mrs Dunne would let them go rather than face her wild daughter again.

'We can't stay here,' she said, 'they're coming after us.'

'We don't know which way to go.'

'Nasfali, I thought you were clever.' She closed her eyes and leaned her head on his shoulder. 'Ask a policeman.'

Of course. 'Drive on, Griffin, until you see a policeman.' He tried to remain very still so that her head would remain just where it was, tucked into the space between his neck and shoulder. He could feel the coldness of all those rings round the top of her right ear.

They crawled jerkily down the darkened streets. Abe's eyes constantly scanned left and right: the windows, the lights, looking for the tell-tale signs that the witches were near them, but all seemed normal.

'Lights ahead, skipper.'

Abe wasn't sure where this skipper business had come from; it sounded like one of those old black and white war films to him, but at least they were taking him seriously now. He wondered what had made them change their minds.

They came to an intersection and a car passed by, and another. Cromwell Road. They slowed down and then stopped. 'And there's a bobby,' said Griffin.

Abe wasn't sure what a bobby was, until he spotted the policeman.

Ten minutes later they were on the dual carriageway, heading out to the motorway, with Griffin whistling through his teeth, and silence from the back. Alicia was awake properly now and she and Abe were locked into a serious discussion about what they should do next. Abe was saying there was no choice. They had the flight all lined up; and surely crossing the ocean would make them safe; and he would find his father and he would look after them all. Alicia said she didn't think his father would be any different to hers and anyway what would stop Abe's mother going out to Egypt, after them. Or, come to think of it, her own mother?

'I thought witches didn't like crossing water,' said Abe.

Alicia shuddered. 'Who does? But you would do it if you had to, wouldn't you?'

'Of course.' Abe frowned. He didn't have any problem crossing water; why should Alicia?

'There you are. Anyway, I'm not giving up.' He had not seen this side of her before; so determined and fired up. She was gripping his hand now, and telling him how she couldn't run, not now. She wanted to find a way to give the team back their lives, all those years they'd lost by being trapped in the picture.

'You can't,' said Abe flatly. 'You can't do that. Nobody can, even your mother knows that, and she knows more than you. You don't even have the knowledge.'

'You saw what I did.' She sat back and withdrew her hand.

'Yes, but you don't know *how* you did that, Alicia. That's wild magic. You don't know where to begin. Let the team come to Egypt; they will have a fantastic time; they will have one great, brilliant moment . . . '

'And then they'll be really old. What then, Nasfali? What will you do for them then? You're thirteen. Will you get a job, will you find a job that will let you look after eleven old men. Are you ready to do that?'

Abe hadn't thought of it like that. No, not at all. 'They'll win the championship. They'll be famous and there'll be my father. I'm going to find my father.'

'Oh, your father again. Even if you find him, is he going to want to look after the boys?'

'We don't need looking after,' said Griffin, as he stared at the road ahead. 'You can just leave us . . . '

Abe felt shamed. Alicia bit her lip. Both of them had forgotten that Griffin was beside them, absorbing everything they were saying. 'I'm sorry,' said Alicia. 'We both want what's best for you; we just don't agree how to do it. Not yet anyway.'

'Sorry, Griffin.'

'That's all right, skipper, me and the team argue all the time. I think this is it, isn't it? Wow.'

The limo was fed into a narrow tunnel and then emerged into a spinning interchange of car parks short-term and long-term and terminals sign-posted every-which-way.

'This one. This one!' They screeched left into a car park, clunked into a space and piled out.

'Safe,' said Abe.

'Don't count on it.' Alicia twisted round to look out of the rear window. 'They're not far,' she said. 'I know they're not.' She lifted her head and sniffed the air, noisily, in a way that was so like her mother that Abe felt almost irritated.

'Well, let's not wait for them.' He immediately rounded up the team and herded them along a walkway into the terminal. Battered and exhausted as they were, the old boys were still overwhelmed by the airport: the endless check-in desks, the bright lights and seething activity even now in the middle of the night, the rattling cafeterias and shops; the arrival and departure screens, and people everywhere, piled up with luggage, singly, in families, with saucer-eyed babies, and scowling teenagers.

'Crikey,' murmured Jissop. 'Crikey. Crikey. Crikey . . . '

Abe had to keep circling them like a sheep dog to stop them just wandering off. Alicia stayed at the back, pushing on the stragglers and keeping an eye behind her.

Eventually they arrived at the Egyptian Air check-in, were greeted by two smart young officials: 'Oh, the team! At last! The embassy gave us all the details. We expected you over an hour ago. Never mind. Is everyone all right? How wonderful you made it; we were worried that you would miss the flight. You'll have to be quick, the flight is scheduled to leave in ten minutes. Thirteen tickets, no luggage. This way. Gate fourteen.'

And they were off again; corridors and walkways, and then just as the team padded their way cautiously on to an escalator, Alicia took Abe's arm and held him back.

'What is it?' he asked.

'I'm not coming.'

'You have to.' He had half suspected she would do this, but he had to stop her. 'They need you. What'll I do about Jonson? And why do you want to stay, Allie?' He had never called her that before. He ignored her raised eyebrow. 'Why? You'll end up having to run from the sisters the whole time. Please come with us.'

'I have to find a way to get to make the men boys again. I have to.' She hesitated. 'And I've felt what it's like, Nasfali, to have power. I've felt it and used it, and I'm going to use it again.'

'But you mustn't. That's what she wants. You'll be like one of them.'

'Excuse me. Do I look like one of them?'

No. She looked pale, serious, and maybe a little sad; she looked too small to be seventeen and having to do battle with her powerful mother; she looked too wild to be wearing that funny, crumpled pink dress; and she looked too beautiful, Abe thought, to leave behind.

'Well do I?' That impatience again.

He shook his head.

'See. I told you I'll be there for the big match. Find your father. Go.'

Abe looked past her, down the wide corridor along which they had just come; it seemed to ripple and shift as if it wasn't made of concrete and steel and covered with carpet; the escalator's quiet hum tightened into a pig-like squeal; and the hard airport light suddenly turned a dusky crimson; and strangest of all, apart from Abe, Alicia, and the team at the top of the escalators, peering anxiously down, there seemed to be no one else in the building.

'They're here, aren't they?'

'Yes, and they'll stop the flight, everything, unless I face them. So go.' She took a deep breath and turned, and as she did so Mrs Dunne emerged out of the blood red shadow at the end of the shifting corridor, and behind her the dark figures of the other sisters.

At least, Abe thought it was them: they looked so different from the way they'd looked at the embassy. Mrs Dunne loomed up to the ceiling, her head bowed because she was too tall to stand straight. Her arms, stretched out on either side, reached halfway down the corridor to them and her face was a vile plum red.

'Allie, come on, you can't fight that!' Abe pleaded, taking a step back and on to the escalator. She looked so small and helpless. 'Alicia, come on!'

But whether it was because of the infernal squealing, just like the ear-splitting noise Abe had heard in his mum's bedroom, or because she was already locked into a mental battle with her monster mother, Alicia didn't turn and didn't answer. She stood, her shoulders drooping slightly, her arms held out a little from her sides, the palms facing forward.

Did she have that awesome power still, or had it been exhausted? Did she know how to summon?

'Alicia!' boomed her mother and all the sisters, their voices as deep and hollow as if they had emerged from the pit of hell.

'Alicia!'

A hot and foul-smelling wind howled down the shifting and twisting corridor, making Allie's pink dress stream back from her legs, and making Abe's eyes water.

Behind him he heard the urgent frightened calling of the team; below, Mrs Dunne's long, sinewy arm now some twenty feet long, it seemed, was reaching past Allie to the escalator itself. Abe, despite his better nature, despite his desire to protect Alicia, was gripped by a feeling of horror. He backed slowly, numbly, up the moving stairs.

Still, Alicia didn't move. Mrs Dunne's hand gripped the black rail of the escalator; Mrs Dunne gave an ear shattering screel and the black rail writhed into the air, cracking over Abe's head like a whip, and then snaking down towards Alicia, looping round and round her, tighter and tighter, till only her head protruded from the black bands of liquorice. The witches swooped closer. Mrs Dunne gave another piercing screel and the escalator juddered to a halt, sending Abe tumbling backwards, so that he cracked his shoulder against the hard edge of the step behind him. Then the escalator began to soften, to melt. The sides poured away into the air, the steps sank like soft mud, and Abe began to slip down into the machine itself.

'Skipper!'

Their faces were horror-struck. For a heartbeat Abe thought that he was gone. Then there was a hand on his, another on his arm, another catching the collar of his jacket. Beneath him, the escalator simply dissolved into liquid that streamed down and down, into a thick darkness from which Mrs Dunne and her kind made their magic.

Suspended for one horrible moment above this abyss, Abe saw the sisters gather round Alicia, his mother right beside Mrs Dunne. He saw them all reach out their left hands as if to touch the girl on the head in some sort of horrid blessing; and then as the team pulled him to safety, he saw Alicia tilt back her head and the same blue lightning he had seen streaming from her fingers now forked out from her eyes. The liquorice-black handrail twisted round her body snapped and cracked and all the sisters, apart from Mrs Dunne, were thrown backwards. Mother and daughter were left facing each other. Then Abe saw Alicia leap cat-like straight at Mrs Dunne and the two toppled into the shaft.

'Allie!'

'Let's go, let's go, it's beginning to happen up here, skipper. The plane! You said . . . ' Griffin hauled Abe back. Roberts took his other arm, Jack pushed and the others ran ahead to the gate as the floorway began to buckle and twist beneath their racing feet.

'Earth tremor,' said the attendant ushering them on to the plane.

'Technical problems,' suggested a steward as the team tumbled down the aisle and flopped into empty seats. The plane began to roll out on to the runway.

Abe closed his eyes and gripped the armrest as the plane started to accelerate.

TWENTY

'This is your captain speaking. You are very welcome aboard this special flight. Our flight time to Cairo airport is exactly five hours forty minutes. We are, at this moment, crossing the English Channel; our flight path will take us . . . '

The rest of the announcement was drowned in a burst of cheers and clapping. Jack and Griffin twirled down the aisle in a loopy waltz, and Abe laughed as the stewardess tried unsuccessfully to usher them back into their seats. The other passengers looked bemused, as well they might seeing these elderly gentlemen pushing and shoving and giggling and hurling the little airline pillows at each other.

'Are they all right?' asked a smart looking woman sitting in the row in front of Abe. 'They look a little strange.'

'They're just happy,' explained Abe. 'Relieved, you know.'

'Ah. They have fear of flying,' she smiled. 'And now they feel safe. I understand.'

'Yes,' said Abe, 'in a manner of speaking.'

They did feel safe. Mrs Dunne was gone and the other witches, his mother included, were left behind. Yes, they were safe, for the moment anyway, but this was small comfort for Abe. He kept seeing, over and over again, Alicia and her mother tumbling into the shaft and spinning and whirling, and flashing with explosions of light as they tumbled down and down, until the sight had been suddenly snatched away from him as the others pulled him away.

He took off his jacket and took the doughnut bag out of his pocket and looked at the money. One thousand pounds. Right then he would have given ten times that amount just to know that Alicia would be able to do as she had promised and come out to them in Cairo. But there was little point in wishing, not now.

'A soft drink?'

The steward held up a can of orange juice.

'Thank you.' Abe took the glass. 'Did you see all that back at the airport?' he asked.

'What was that?'

'The explosions and damage to the escalators. Didn't anyone report anything or any of your crew see anything?'

'I don't think so, sir. Sometimes airports and late night travelling can be quite disorientating. I wouldn't worry . . . '

No. Of course, no one would ever know anything. That was their power; their world threaded the world of ordinary people and yet somehow remained apart from it, and what they didn't want seen, or known, or remembered would never be seen, or known, or remembered. The thought made him feel, really for the first time in his life, very alone.

The main cabin lights had dimmed and gradually, one by one, the individual lights clicked off. The euphoria the team felt at their escape and the sheer excitement of being on a plane and being offered food on a little plastic tray in little plastic containers was all too much for them and Abe saw that every one of them was fast asleep.

Abe closed his eyes. How was he going to manage? How was he going to manage in a foreign land with Jonson ill and no one to help? The image of his father stepping out into a crowded street, looking back and smiling, slipped momentarily across his mind's eye. My father the criminal, he thought. My father the forger.

PART THREE
TO GO LOOKING IN CAIRO

TWENTY-ONE

'Hello, my name is Jamil. Come this way, please. This way. You had a good flight? This way. A few questions. We have it arranged. I am the press officer, you see. Through here now.' Jamil was small, brisk, and neat. He swept them into a room with blue square furniture, and white stone floors. Bright early morning light flooded in through the lattice slats of the airport blinds but this was pulverized by the bright flashes of the cameras.

'Just a few questions,' the smooth-talking press secretary had said, instinctively addressing his remarks to Griffin, who grinned and grunted and poked Abe discreetly whenever he could. Griffin, as always, seemed to be enjoying himself; the others less so: Roberts had swollen feet; Gannet felt faint; Jack was red-faced and puffy; and Jonson's bald head streamed with perspiration.

They were ranged along a narrow table and the press and one camera crew faced them. Mr Jamil was in the middle and beside him was a neat looking man with a trimmed black beard and dark eyes who said very little but was apparently the first minister for sport. Abe, tucked out of the way at the far end of the table, worried how the team would behave with the press.

The questions streamed up at the bemused boys who sat wrinkle faced, and muggy from the heat and jet lag.

'Can you play? You look a little past it, if you don't mind me saying.' That was a local paper. A young woman journalist.

'Who do you play first?' An important national daily.

'How long have you played together?'

'Are you fit? How often do you train? . . . ' And so it went on.

They did their best.

'Past it!' said Roberts. 'We biffed Brazil . . . '

'Excuse me, what is "biffed"?'

Roberts ignored the question. ' . . . and we gave the Americans the old heave-ho. Didn't we, chaps?'

'I'll say we did!'

'Heave ho?' said the puzzled important national daily.

Griffin stood up. 'He means,' he said in his most serious and most pompous voice, 'that we have been entirely victorious and I think I can say,' he continued, looking theatrically around at the team, 'that that is exactly how we intend to carry on.'

'Griffin,' said Bittern solemnly, 'you may be a prune but that was a tiptop speech.'

The others showed their approval by thumping the table with their fists.

Jamil looked worried.

'And your first match is with whom?'

'Don't know who we're playing. Our manager would know that.'

Jonson suddenly stood up. 'Back in a jiffy,' he muttered and bolted from the room.

'Old waterworks,' said Thomas glumly, 'giving him a bit of a problem.'

'Who is your manager? Which of you . . . ?'

'That's him there, the skipper,' said Griffin pointing at Abe. 'He does the planning. It was all his idea, this championship business. He's jolly cunning. Miss Dunne too.' The others nodded and murmured their agreement.

The journalists looked blank for a moment and then because every single one of these strange elderly men turned towards the boy, the cameras swung round and popped at Abe.

Cunning as a fox, thought Abe, blinking rapidly against the lights, a desert fox.

'You are a very young boy. How can you look after grown men? This is not possible . . . '

'Anything is possible,' said Abe. 'You just have to know what you want and then plan carefully in order to get it.'

One or two of the journalists laughed outright. The young woman journalist smiled.

'He's a top schemer,' announced Jack. 'You wait and see.'

'And his dad is here,' added Stokely but no one paid any attention to what he said because at that moment the first minister of sport, who had sat there saying absolutely nothing, suddenly stood up. 'This young man,' he said indicating Abe, 'has my every confidence. Thank you, gentlemen.' And that was it. The journalists closed their notebooks, put away their microphones, the first minister, closely followed by Mr Jamil, swept out of the room. The conference was over.

Jack did his first camel impression.

Abe stretched, then went over to Griffin. 'Thank you. It was very nice what you said.'

'Cunning,' said Griffin. 'Could we get Big Macs now?'

'What! You must be joking. It's serious training from now on.'

Jamil came with them on the coach to the hotel and as they swung through the streets of Cairo, their driver blasting his horn and cutting a swathe through the early morning traffic, he rattled through their itinerary: the practices, photo shoots, and little trips to the bazaars for shopping and more photo shoots. The team ignored him: they yawned and scratched themselves. Outside Cairo streamed by: cars and scooters, bright colours, flowing robes, western suits . . . I'm home, thought Abe. It was a strange feeling.

A few minutes into their journey, Thomas squeezed past Mr Jamil to speak to Abe.

'Jonno is not at all good, skipper. Will this man here,' giving Jamil a nod, 'get him a doctor, do you think?'

Abe promised they would have a doctor as soon as they reached their hotel and Thomas squeezed back to his seat.

'Of course, I will have a doctor come immediately but will they be able to play in the match, do you think? We have all this arranged. It is too late, too difficult to change things. The Italians are sending a team in six days. The great inaugural match is the next day.'

Forty minutes later, they were all gathered in Abe's room, all apart from Jonson who was being seen by the hotel doctor. They looked worried.

'You must be cheerful,' said Abe. 'Jonson will be all right. Think of it: you're going to be on world news, TV, everything. You will be footballers of fame, desert dervishes; players of the pyramids.' He looked around at them. They didn't like Jonson being sick, of course they didn't, but instead of being reassured by the arrival of the doctor, it had really unsettled them.

'Who wants to play against a bunch of old men?'

'Old Italians.'

'It'll be too easy,' yawned Jack. He had his legs hooked over the side of his chair and was swinging them up and down, and poking Bittern each time he did so. Bittern was too fed up to react; he just joggled a little each time Jack's foot poked him.

'My feet hurt all the time,' said Roberts. 'I don't think it will be easy at all.'

'This is going to be a world championship. You'll be playing professionals. You'll train.' They groaned. 'Don't worry, you'll be great.'

'What about Jonno,' said Chivers. Everyone looked at Abe. 'He might not be well enough to play. Then what? We'll only be ten . . . '

Roberts whispered something to Griffin, who nodded. 'Where's your dad, skipper?'

'Yes,' echoed the others. 'Where is he?'

'I don't know. I have to find him. I will though and I know he'll help.'

'Skipper, your mother was one of Mrs Dunne's . . . ' Griffin hesitated, 'one of her people.'

'He means she was a witch.'

'Like Miss Dunne's mum.'

They were all pitching in now.

'And Miss Dunne could do things.'

'Like at the aerodrome . . . '

'And the embassy. Do you remember that . . . '

'Yes.'

'So can't you do things too, skipper?'

'Me?'

They nodded.

'I don't know.'

'You let us out.'

'I don't know, but I thought my father might be able to. I think he can. I thought he might be like my mother, only different, better . . . '

There was a knock at the door. Jissop opened it and the young, businesslike hotel doctor came in. 'Ah,' he said, 'your friend. Who should I speak to?'

'I think you had better speak to us all,' said Abe. 'We all want to know.'

The doctor ignored him. 'Is there anyone in charge?'

'You heard the skipper,' said Jack from his chair. 'Spill the beans, old boy.'

'I see. Your friend is very ill. I am sorry. He needs to be kept still. I have given him something which will make him comfortable, and I will arrange twenty-four hour care. It will be expensive but . . . ' he raised his hands, 'what can one do? It is the will of God.'

'I have money,' said Abe.

'It may not be necessary,' said the doctor. 'I will speak with Mr Jamil.' And he gave a little bow and backed out of the room.

There was a stunned silence.

Griffin was the first to speak. 'We'll have to play as a ten-man team,' he said. 'He would want that.'

They nodded their agreement and then looked at Abe.

'And I,' said Abe, 'will find my father.' He stood up. 'All *will* be well.'

'That's the ticket, skipper.'

That evening Abe began his search. A lottery ticket seller, a man in a loose white suit sipping tea from a thimble-sized glass, and a news-vendor watched idly as the young boy hurried out of the Hotel Luxor and, after only a few minutes' hesitation, like a diver on the edge of a river bank, plunged into the city.

TWENTY-TWO

Cars, bazaars, the great Nile, wide and flat, and here, where it slowly flowed past the steaming streets of the city, brown and slack as a dull desert snake. All the pictures he'd had plastered around the walls of his bedroom a thousand miles away in London blazed into sudden life but Abe had no time for gazing and dreaming and wondering; he hurried, all the time he hurried. Cairo was so huge. The mother of all cities, so said the hotel porter. 'The mother of all cities and you seek your father. Only in Cairo could this happen.'

Where should Abe begin?

Away from the central boulevards and squares, out of the streaming, squealing traffic, down the narrower roads, the smaller streets, looking all the time for some glimpse that would remind him of that image he had of his father stepping out into that street. He had the photograph, but what could it tell him? The streets all looked the same to him and there were so many people: people selling and bartering, hurrying and dawdling, arguing, sitting and smoking and watching. People in doorways, hanging on the backs of buses, carrying boxes, lugging jerrycans, or selling lottery tickets.

Abe was everywhere. He saw everything, but he found . . .

Nothing.

He went further. He scoured the old part of the city. He jumped on a bus and headed out through half-built slabs of apartments, grey and dusty, washing draped from windows, rubble-strewn yards, pot-holed roads, and crop-haired boys yelling and playing football.

A routine developed: while Abe searched, the team trained and Jonson, propped up on his bed, received detailed updates how each day's training had gone; that is to say, as soon as the team piled off the coach they burst in on him, an explosion of bandy knees and bony elbows, little paunches and wide grins.

'Should've seen me, Jonno, did a brilliant header.'

'It's stingy when you're bald!'

'I ate six kebaby things,' crowed Jack. 'Don't tell the skipper.'

But Abe did keep an eye on the boys. He spoke to the trainer every day, he reported to Mr Jamil who was in touch with the minister, and made a point of being back at the hotel when they returned from their training.

He also thought constantly of Alicia and tried his best to do what she would have wanted. Sometimes he believed that she had escaped from her mother; after all, her mother had never meant to kill her. And if she had escaped perhaps, just perhaps, she would keep her promise.

Four days passed by.

Apart from Jonson, the boys were fit and kept so busy thoughts of family and home didn't appear to bother them; they all talked constantly of the big match, less than a week away. Every day Griffin and Jack devised some new trick to stun their opponents: the synchronized hip wiggle, the highland twirl, and Griffin's favourite, the Maori war face where they all stuck out their tongues and rolled their eyeballs.

'Do we look very beastly?' Stokely asked Abe after their practice on day five.

'Very beastly,' agreed Abe.

Before going to bed, they asked Abe if he had had any news of his dad and Abe had to admit that no, he hadn't but they weren't to worry, all would be well.

On the sixth day, worn out, he bought a cold Coke from a street vendor, found himself a patch of shade and sat and sipped the Coke. This was so far from what he had dreamed about: hot gritty dust swirled round him, and caked his lips. Moonlight rides on the back of a camel, high dunes and mysterious pyramids, and Alicia . . . He swirled the Coke in his mouth and spat.

'Baksheesh.'

A small boy with yellowy curly hair and ragged clothes stood in front of him with a hand out. 'Give me money for a Coke.'

'Why?'

'Because,' explained the boy, 'you have money. You have Coke. I don't. You are not Egyptian. See, I speak English because I know you are not Egyptian. Money.' He poked his hand at Abe.

'What's your name?'

'Cyrus. Money.'

'My father's Egyptian,' said Abe. 'Here.' He tipped three coins into the boy's hand. 'No, wait,' he said as the yellow-haired boy immediately started to run off. 'Wait, I want to ask you something.'

'What is it?'

Suspicious, the boy turned back.

'Where would you hide,' asked Abe, 'not for a game but if you wanted to run away from your home, your parents? If you wanted to run from the police even. Where would you be safe?'

The boy looked at him with solemn eyes. 'Are you wanting to hide?'

'I am looking for someone.'

'Your brother?'

'No.' Abe smiled. 'My father.'

The boy nodded. 'Necropolis,' he said.

'What's that?'

'Necropolis, city of the dead.' He shrugged. 'Many many people there and they have no papers, no work, nothing, but they live.'

Yes! The hair prickled on the nape of his neck. City of the dead, of course. 'And what of the dead?' asked Abe. 'You said it was a city of the dead.'

'Yes. It was built for the dead. Many dead there. They don't mind. Maybe your father is there.' He ran off a few paces and then stopped again. 'If he is dead, he will surely be there.'

Abe stood up and eagerly began to retrace his steps into the city. His father wasn't dead. He wasn't; but he might hide among the dead, mightn't he?

He bought a guide book. Then he called in to Jonson and talked with him for a little while.

'I want to play.'

'Perhaps.'

'No,' said Jonson, 'you don't understand.' He gripped Abe's hand. 'I want to play. I want something to look forward to.'

Abe turned a little away from him. 'All right, you will play. I promise you will.' Another promise. He imagined Alicia giving a sniff of disapproval. Perhaps they should take him out to the desert and bury him up to the neck with his promises. 'Don't worry.'

Jonson smiled and Abe left the room.

He met Jamil in the hotel lobby delivering boxes of clothes for the team: white cotton tracksuits with *Egypt* imprinted on the back in bold red letters. Then he went up to his room and read. Yes, there was such a place, a necropolis it was called and, said the guide book, it was inhabited. In fact it was thriving; hundreds of little businesses operated there amid the tombs and sarcophogi. He would go there the next day.

Later, as usual, he met the team in a little drawing room where they had tea and watched the news. They were sitting round the television when he came in, eating ice creams and talking quietly. 'Here, look at this!' exclaimed Jissop. 'It's the team. Look at them.'

It was the arrival of the Italians. They were filmed

stepping down from the plane and then again coming out of the main terminal and boarding their coach.

'They don't look that decrepit, do they?'

Indeed they didn't. They looked sleek: smooth grey hair, healthy tanned faces, all in neat double-breasted blazers. '*Viva Italia*,' they said, smiling and waving to the camera.

'Viva beaver,' sneered Jack, shovelling the end bit of his cone into his mouth.

The new outfits were brought up, tried on, and the next day, instead of heading off on his own, Abe accompanied them to the expensive stadium where they were training with an Egyptian coach.

'How are they doing?' he asked.

'Sometimes good; sometimes silly. They are like children.' He shook his head. 'Men in Egypt are not like this.'

Abe watched them run up and down and then had the odd feeling of someone staring at him. Unsettled, he glanced over his shoulder and sniffed the dry air. What was it?

'Why not let them play footballers their own age?' A man in a crumpled white suit whom Abe had half noticed hanging around down at the goal had drifted over to stand beside him and the trainer. The question was casual; the voice, low and somehow musical, but it startled Abe. He stared at the man. Why did he seem familiar? 'Look at them,' said the man, 'they're bored.' The team had, in fact, given up and in ones and twos came over to Abe. 'See,' he said, 'they want fun. Don't you, boys?'

'We want a bally ice cream, that's what.'

'Training's boring.'

The trainer threw up his hands and stalked off, muttering to himself.

'What do you mean, with players their own age?' said Abe. 'They've a match in a couple of days against a professional team of senior players. Is that what you mean?'

The man shook his head. 'No. I don't mean they should play old men at all. But boys their own age. You know what I mean.'

How did he know they were boys?

There was a stir of agreement from the team. 'Footer in the street. Can we?' They jostled and shoved and were their old selves. 'All right,' said Abe. 'I know just where to go.' When he looked up to thank the man, he'd gone. Strange. And it was strange that he should call the team boys, as if he knew that beneath the wrinkles and paunches that is exactly what they were. Abe shrugged away the thought and led them all back to the coach.

Abe guided the coach driver on a tour of the back streets until, more by luck than design, they found their way into the area Abe had been in the day before, and there, sure enough, was the same gang of boys he'd seen, playing street football.

'Here you are,' said Abe. 'The coach will come back and pick you up at four.'

As the coach slowly reversed out of the cul-de-sac, Abe watched the two groups confront each other. One of the street children had scooped up their ball and held it under his arm. His mates gathered around, waiting to see what these elderly foreigners were up to. They didn't have to wait long. Griffin suddenly gave a whoop, tossed down his shoulder bag with the expensive football boots in it, and ran straight up to the boy with the ball. Whether he said something or not, Abe had no way of telling but the next instant the ball was high in the air, and the team had ranged out into position. They looked happy.

'Where now?' asked the driver.

'Necropolis,' said Abe.

'OK.'

TWENTY-THREE

The driver left him at a wide and unpromising crossroads. 'You go up that way,' he said in his hoarse and rather high voice. 'Not good to take my coach there. I lose wheels, seats, everything. Too many thief. Up that way. It's very big. You know what you are looking for?'

Abe knew.

'Not good to get lost. Don't miss your big match tomorrow.' And with that warning the driver hauled the coach round and headed back into the city. Abe turned about and trudged up a featureless road with the same little workshops and buildings half built and abandoned that he had seen in other run-down parts of Cairo.

Where did the city of the living end and the city of the dead begin? It seemed all one, except the street narrowed, and the buildings became squat, more cramped together and some had iron grilles over the windows, and some had pots and dishes, and plastic flowers placed in the doorways; and when he asked a man where was the city of the dead, the man just gave a jerk of his head. 'Up here. This is the dead. All around you.'

Indeed Necropolis sprawled around him in a maze of streets and blind alleys, plots of graves, stately mausoleums, family tombs, and those little houses he had already noticed, built for the dead though families had moved into some of these. People must live, he said to himself. People must live. And he thought of poor Jonson, his face bandage-white, in that dusky cool hotel room.

He passed through an area where tinsmiths worked, and then he was aware of gypsies, dark, dark skin and bright clothes.

Would his father keep his name? How would he live?

The sun beat down and Abe's head throbbed. There was so little time, how could he find him? A needle in a haystack, that would be easier, so much easier, one piece of hay at a time, but this ancient city had no beginning and for sure there was no end. He saw an opening into a shady dirt garden, a graveyard patch with scanty grass and baked earth, and a single tree with brittle leaves that cast a welcome shade. He sat and hunched up his knees and ignored a skinny dog that scuttled in, sniffed him, and then lay down beside him.

What would he do, if he were a forger? Where in this place would he go? Abe scratched idly in the dirt while he wondered. A forger was an artist, wasn't he, a maker? There had to be an area for craftsmen like that: carving on tombs, all that metal work he had seen, engraved inscriptions. He set off with renewed hope and when he asked if he'd find engravers anywhere he was told yes and was directed further along. Yes, yes, the men, the children, the bad-tempered guides who darted out from the more ornate mausoleums wanting baksheesh to show him around, yes, yes, they said, many engravers, further along . . .

The sun slipped down, and suddenly, because there were no street lights, it was completely dark. He stumbled on for a little, occasionally there was the flicker of light from a chink in a door or window, or a blaze where a family gathered around a fire, but in between he tripped and fell and groped along walls, until, exhausted, he crawled under what he thought was a table, curled up and went to sleep.

He woke in a grey pre-dawn light with a sharp pain in the small of his back and when he sat up he banged his head not on wood but stone. He stiffly rolled out of his sleeping space.

'The sleep of the dead, eh!' chuckled a grizzled looking beggar squatting on his haunches and smoking a cigarette down to its glowing butt. 'Resurrection, eh? Dead coming up; dead going down.' He clearly could have continued in that vein all day but Abe interrupted him, asking where was the alley of the engravers. 'I will show you,' said the beggar, eyeing him thoughtfully. 'You have a coin? Two coins?' Abe handed over the money. 'You must have a powerful charm, sleeping out like that with money in your pocket. Do you have more? These two little coins are not so much for guiding you . . . ' He stepped closer to Abe, one hand held out, the other sliding under his ragged shirt at the back, reaching for something.

'No!' Abe barked, stabbing a pointed finger at the man. 'Do not even think you can rob me.' He was angry but he didn't know why he had reacted like that; it had been automatic, but it had worked.

The man winced, as if he had been stung. 'I merely asked, young pasha,' he whined. 'I do not want your money. Come, I will show you what you seek,' and he scuttled off down the alley and Abe had to hurry to catch up with him.

Clearly Abe had given the beggar a fright. Good. 'Have you heard of an engraver called Ma'halli?'

The man looked at him sideways. 'Perhaps. There are many here. Look, this is your street.' Before Abe could thank him, he was gone.

Close.

His heart thumped like a war drum as he climbed an outside stairway to the top floor of a little workshop where a burly engraver had said, yes, a man worked there who called himself Ma'halli, sometimes, and he had laughed. 'Names change, only death is constant,' he said.

Abe was getting tired of asking anyone anything. 'Everyone's a philosopher here,' he muttered to himself as he knocked on the door.

No reply, of course. He took a deep breath and tried the handle. The door was unlocked. He had come so far, surely it was all right to step inside and have a look. He braced himself and stepped in.

The room was almost bare, whitewashed, square with a table, a chair, a narrow box-bed on one side and a single window, with no covering or glass, through which the already hot sun streamed. Was there nothing there to tell him about the owner of that room; anything to suggest it really might belong to this man, his father?

There were scratches on the wall by the window, as if someone had sat on the chair looking out, ticking off the days. The last scratch, a neat line like all the others, had a circle etched round it. He ran his hand over the table, under the bed. Nothing. But when he turned back towards the door, he saw something he had missed: a card, no a picture, a photograph, an old one, small, on the floor. How could he have missed it?

He suddenly found himself sniffing again. What was happening? He'd only ever sniffed when he'd had a cold but now he seemed to have turned into a bloodhound. It reminded him of Mrs Dunne, of his mother, and then Alicia too. What was it? Something he had sensed before? He sniffed again so loudly that he was surprised at himself, the thick hot air whistling up his nose. And again he had an almost tangible sense of someone, someone he knew, being close by. He stooped and picked up the photograph.

It was of a young woman, very beautiful with dark hair and a serious face. She stared straight up at him, and the drumming in his chest gave him such a hard wallop that he sat down on the chair with a jolt. His mother. This was the place; this really was it.

'Can I help you?'

Abe didn't turn around, not straight away. He gripped the edge of the table and closed his eyes, forcing his voice to be steady. 'I don't know,' he said. 'Can you?' Then he turned and squinted at the figure framed in the bright light of the doorway.

'This is my room. I do not expect boys to come into my room. Oh . . . ' The voice was low and had a musical quality that reminded Abe of the odd man in the stadium who had suggested the team play with boys; but as the man came into the room, and Abe could make out his features more clearly, he wasn't entirely sure that it was him. It could have been; he just wasn't sure. The clothes were the same: crumpled white jacket, collarless shirt, cotton trousers, also white.

'It's you,' said the man as if it were exactly Abe whom he had expected to turn up.

'You know who I am?'

'Of course. You are famous. Television. The football team. Those old men. It was your idea they say, to hold this world championship for—what do they call them—senior citizens. Egypt loves the idea. Your name is Ebrahim Nasfali. You have been in Cairo six days. I have seen you many times.'

'Ebrahim Nasfahl Ma'halli is my full name but I have lived in Britain all my life. They can't cope with names like that there. They call me Abe or Nasfali.'

'I see. You have brought no one here with you?'

'No. Are you the man they call Ma'halli?'

It was like a polite tennis match.

The man nodded. 'This is so.'

How do you ask a stranger if he is your father, thought Abe? You don't. You wait because a father should come to the child.

'Is this yours?' Abe held out the photograph. 'Did you know her?'

'Maybe.'

'She's my mother.'

'Ah.'

Abe stood up. 'I came here to find my father because I need him to help me.' A fly buzzed in front of his face and he flapped it away. 'I have come a long way and . . . ' the words caught in his throat and he had to swallow and start again, 'and I have lost someone I liked very much.' He paused. 'And I have another friend who is very, very sick.'

197

'No one can escape death.'

'I know,' said Abe. 'I know it is all around us.'

The man, for the first time, smiled. 'This is true.' He held out his hand. 'Give me the picture, Ebrahim.' Abe handed over the photograph. 'And the other you have, yes?'

Slowly Abe pulled out the scratched photograph with the blank space where a man had stood and smiled.

The man seemed far from surprised. 'Ah yes. You found this. You don't know how grateful I am.'

'You are him, aren't you? You are my father?' He knew it; of course he did, but he still wanted it said.

'I am. There. Are you happy, Ebrahim? You have found me and you want my help. This is only fair since you saved me.' He gazed keenly at Abe for a moment. 'Yes. You knew that, didn't you?' Abe nodded. There were no embraces or hugs, none of that soppy film nonsense. How could there be; they were father and son . . . and strangers. 'So, if I am to help your friend, we must go, and quickly.'

Abe looked at his watch. It was only eight in the morning, but the match was that night. The team would be fretting if he wasn't there and it had taken hours to work his way through this strange city. 'I'm ready,' he said.

'Good. Wait outside.'

Abe followed his father down the stairs and then waited while he swept a dusty red sheet from a gleaming black and chrome motorcycle. 'Harley Davidson,' he said. 'Yes?'

He might as well have said British Rail for all it meant to Abe, and when Abe made no response his father said: 'Your mother has much to answer for.' Then he picked up a petrol can and ran back up the stairs. Abe could see him slopping it about. Then he stood in the doorway, took out a Zippo lighter, flipped the top and struck the wheel. He tossed the burning lighter into the room, vaulted over the stair rail and landed lightly on his feet beside Abe, just as a ball of flame burst out of the room above them. Then he was on the bike and kicking it alive. 'Quick. Behind me.'

Abe scrambled up on to the back, hesitated for a moment then put his arms round his father's waist. Then the engine roared, the back wheel spun for a moment in the dirt, and they were off, slithering round the first corner and down a winding alley where the first people were already out, visiting their dead or busy selling. Behind them a thin black plume of smoke rose straight up into the windless sky.

'Why did you do that?'

'You have betrayed me,' shouted his father. 'You saved me; then you betrayed me.' He laughed, swooped round a lorry, and squealed to a stop at a traffic light. 'And both times you did not know what you were doing.'

'I am not stupid.'

'No. No. But she will follow you to find me.'

'Mrs Dunne is dead.'

'No, not Mrs Dunne, your mother, boy, your mother. I know she will follow me and try to trap me. She will look for you too.'

'I don't think so. She never liked me much.'

His father laughed. 'She never liked me either but that won't stop her.'

'Did you love her?'

'Of course.'

'Then why does she want to trap you again?'

'She cannot help herself, Ebrahim. She must hunt me as the spider must hunt the fly. And when the fly is caught will the spider let it go again? No. She cannot let go. It is not in her nature.'

'She never loved you at all?'

'No. Love was a trick she played. She cannot love, Ebrahim. She doesn't feel the same things that you and I feel. Except maybe hunger. She and those others like her have a terrible hunger. It eats at them. This is all they think, all they feel, and it is hunger for power, Ebrahim, this is all they desire.' Abe's father's head was half turned so that his words would carry over the noise of the traffic, and Abe, studying that profile, wondered why his mother should have singled him out, a forger, she had said, a thief. 'This is why she kept me trapped, so she could feed off me. Year after year, so little by little I grow weaker. But not now, eh! Now, I am free and she must look for me.'

The lights changed and Abe had to cling tight as they tilted back on to their rear wheel and howled through the intersection and down into the city.

TWENTY-FOUR

All his life Abe had longed to see Cairo and now here he was with his arms clasped round his father's waist and his eyes tight shut as they swayed and dipped and soared, threading round trams, and vans, and cars, and crowds of people, never slowing, it seemed, always moving swiftly like a bird catching the currents of the air.

'Here.'

The hotel. His father somehow a little taller, distinguished flecks of grey in his black hair that Abe had not noticed before, striding ahead of him, slapping the dust from the white suit which in the full light of the morning looked crisp and clean and decidedly elegant. The porter ducked his head and swung open the glass door, murmuring, 'This way, Pasha.' Abe, hurrying after him, felt shabby and self-conscious.

'You're different.'

'No. I am the same.' He smiled gravely. 'Appearance, Ebrahim, is always a deceptive thing.' The lift door slid open and they stepped on to the blue carpet of the fourth floor. 'Sometimes, it helps if I let people see what they expect. You know?' He smoothed his hair and the grey had gone. He laughed. 'It is nothing. You will learn. Do you remember a man standing by the hotel entrance on your first day here? No? At the stadium? I needed to see, Ebrahim, if you were my son, or hers.'

'And?'

His father shrugged. 'I think you are your own person, Ebrahim, and this is as it should be.'

Jonson's room was in half darkness, his round face, gleaming pale and moonlike, stared dully at the ceiling. Both hands clutched the edge of his sheet which he had pulled up as far as his thin chest. His arms looked so thin too, the muscles wasting so quickly, leaving slack skin.

They sat on either side of him, and Abe's father gently prised one hand away from the sheet and held it for a moment. Dimly they could hear the traffic of Cairo in the distance, but in the room, all Abe was aware of was Jonson's hurried, shallow breathing.

'He will not live to see the Great Pyramid or his team mates play their game.' His father's voice was soft, almost as if he were talking to himself. 'His death draws very near. I can hear the horses of night coming closer. Listen.'

Abe leaned forward but he heard no horses. Instead he saw Jonson's fingers tighten their grip on the damp sheet, and heard a catch in his in-drawn breath. He saw the lids of his closed eyes tremor and then open and he saw his lips move and when he bent lower he heard the anxiety in his faint voice.

'Miss Alicia promised she'd come for me.'

'Shush now,' said Abe's father. 'Many things are promised. Many.'

Whether this was meant to be a comfort or not, Abe couldn't tell. Poor Jonson, his breathing was so light and fine it sounded like the fluttering of birds' wings.

'We cannot defeat his death; it already feeds on him but perhaps we can postpone it.' He smiled. 'Cheat a little.'

Abe's breath caught in his throat. 'You mean you can turn back time, turn back the clock. Is that what you mean?' Just like Alicia! That's what she'd said she was going to try to do. If it was really possible then perhaps everything could be undone; like winding back a video. Perhaps his father could make it so that Alicia and Mrs Dunne had never had that terrible fight at the airport.

'No,' said his father sharply and then lowered his head, as if ashamed, and held up his hands. 'All I can do now is cheat a little. This is it.'

Of course, Abe thought dully. His father was a forger, a cheat. Alicia was gone, Jonson would go, but maybe if he could help a little, that would be something. 'How can you help him?'

'Death hungers for life. If we add to your friend's store of life, death will come, but more slowly.' Abe's father looked across at him. 'Ebrahim,' he said, 'nothing comes from nothing.'

'I know that. It is the first law of business.'

'So how much would you give to your friend? How much of your life would you give?'

'My life?'

'Of course.'

'Can you do that?'

'Of course. You give a couple of years, he lives a little longer; you live a little shorter but you lose nothing now, only when you are older. It is not so terrible. Better to give, than have your time taken from you. My time was taken from me, Ebrahim, thirteen years, your childhood.'

Abe frowned. What kind of a man was his father? Was he like Abe, ordinary, maybe with schemes that had got him into trouble, like Abe's often had? An innocent bystander who had just got caught up in some business of Abe's mother's and had then been thrust aside, like she had cast him into that rubbish strewn underworld? Or was he something else? How could he really trust him until he knew. 'Tell me now, why she did this to you?'

'Because she is a thief,' he said flatly, 'and she wanted to steal from me, Ebrahim, and that is what she did. There was a time when I had more knowledge than any man, a lifetime learning and my father before me, and his before him. With knowledge comes power. Then I had more power than her and all her kind; but it was knowledge I hungered for. And then she came and I loved her and couldn't see her for what she was.' A slight shrug. 'A trick. Crude magic that I could have swept aside had I been watchful. And then suddenly there are newspaper reports and police investigations and she has made the world believe I am a criminal. So I am in real prison: walls of brick and high windows with iron bars and little light for thirteen years. But she did this.'

Abe nodded. Yes, they could do that. They could twist things like the way Mrs Dunne had made it seem the team had died when the train blew up.

'And because she had a part of me, locked away somewhere safe, she could feed on me, and slowly, little by little, year by year, steal from me the things I knew. Now she has almost all my power,' he gave a short laugh, 'but she doesn't know how to use it. If she or others of her kind ever do learn, the world will become a terrible place for they will bring only darkness.'

'The witches of Britain.'

'If only they would stay there,' grunted his father, 'but she will come. She must find me and when she does she will try to make me teach her. And she will find me . . . but not yet. Not yet, Ebrahim, for we have much to do.'

He tried to tell his father about the great battle at the airport and how Alicia had saved them all. How all the witches were destroyed. He was sure of it, pulled down when Mrs Dunne and her daughter fell together into the long dark shaft.

His father listened closely but still shook his head. 'It may be so but remember, Ebrahim, what you see is sometimes what they wish you to see. I think, I feel she is coming. I feel we have little time. Now, if you wish to do this thing for your friend I will help; if you do not I will not think the worse of you. Decide.'

Abe looked down at Jonson. Poor old Jonson. He seemed to remember him always smiling but with little to say. He and Thomas were friends, weren't they, Jonson a little in the other's shadow. But what did he know of him really?

'Ebrahim. Time.'

What did he know of any of the team? Just that they

were boys like him but old. They were his responsibility. He had released them, freed them; and he had promised them . . . Many things are promised . . . His father had just said that, hadn't he? So how could he turn his back now? He couldn't. That was it. 'He must come to the match,' Abe said finally. 'Take what you need.'

His father looked at him. 'So generous,' he said, 'and that is a good thing. Here, take his hand.'

Abe did as he was told. Jonson's old hand rested lightly in his. Was that it? No knife, no incision, no tubes and red blood pumping around in little spirals of plastic? Only this? And yet, just as he was questioning the very plain nature of this moment, he felt something shift. It was as if the room was receding; the walls further away; the bed smaller, and Jonson too; and quite suddenly, for just a fleeting moment, he was able to see himself, his father, and the frail man in the bed all beneath him. Abe felt a momentary weariness, and a tightening of the skin on his face, and then he was once again himself, beside the bed, watching the colour return to Jonson's cheek, and his head lifting from the pillow.

'Now,' said his father, 'quickly, we must go,' and he put an arm around the back of Jonson's neck and helped him sit, and then swing his legs out. 'Clothes, Ebrahim. Ebrahim!'

Abe shook himself. It was one thing to hear his father talk; it was quite another to see the dying Jonson sitting up with that smile creeping back into his face. He looked at his father. His father the forger, the cheat. 'You did this!'

'We.'

'You're not just a . . . '

'Forger? Thief? No, I have a little power, enough to . . . '

' . . . Cheat.'

'Yes.'

And at that moment, it was as if a barrier between father and son had been passed. There was time for a fleeting smile and then quickly they dressed Jonson. When they were finished, he stood up, took a deep breath and to Abe's enquiry, said: 'I feel fine. Wizard, in fact. Is this your dad? Very nice to meet you,' and he held out his hand and the two men shook. 'Do you think I will be able to play? I think I might.'

'You might,' said Abe, 'but we need to hurry. How do we get to Giza, father?'

'Since we cannot fly, we must drive.'

It was only when they were sitting in the back of a cab, that Jonson seemed to focus on Abe. He stared at him so hard that Abe asked him what the matter was. 'It's not me, skipper, it's you. You're different. What happened to you?'

'He's a little older,' said his father, 'two years, maybe three. He does not mind, do you, Ebrahim?'

Fifteen, maybe sixteen. No, he didn't mind. It made him think of Alicia though. How long ago it seemed that he had hung on the radiator and dreamed silly, childish dreams of riding in the desert with her, she with the rings and the wild spiky hair.

'Can it really take this long?'

For four hours they drove and the city seemed to stretch for ever.

'I cannot make Cairo's traffic disappear. Be patient,' he said calmly. 'There is an end to every journey.' But Abe noticed how his father's fingers endlessly drummed a nervous tattoo on the arm rest.

'I don't know that I will be much use in the match,' said Jonson. 'I don't feel so strong really. Do you think they brought some kit out for me?'

'We'll find something,' said Abe.

And then quite suddenly it was as if Cairo simply let go. 'See,' said Abe's father, 'desert.'

Instead of houses and shacks, there were scrubby

roadside fields, the soil burned and stony, and rising up before them was the barren land of the desert; open, bare, shimmering with heat and dust, and, suddenly, unexpectedly there, towering over this emptiness, the man-made mountains, the pyramids of Giza: Cheops, Chephren, Mycerinius. Abe rolled the hard heavy names round in his mind. The photographs plastered on his bedroom wall faded. Here was the solid unbelievable reality. Stone block placed on stone, placed on stone. Great blocks levelled and squared, heaved, hoisted, and lowered. A barrier against the desert, or against the city of men? A frontier between life and death, or perhaps a challenge to the gods?

The three peaks, sharp, angled at the vastness of the desert sky as if they could somehow fall upwards and punch a hole through the blue dome and tumble into space to drift among the stars.

'You chose this place, Ebrahim?'

He had. 'Yes.' He glimpsed a tourist office off to the left, and people everywhere, traders, and robed dealers, and frowning pale men and women, clutching cameras; and a smell, not the hot fumes of traffic, but the sweet thick stench of stables. But all the time, as they drew slowly closer, his eyes were drawn to the Great Pyramid. There were crowds swarming around the base, tiny, insignificant, hustling and hurrying.

'Can you feel it?' said his father. 'Ka. The life force. This is a place of power, but perhaps you knew that?'

'I . . . I don't know. Yes, I suppose so.' Abe pulled a face. 'That's what all the books say but I didn't choose it for that reason. I just wanted to see it. I don't know why. It seemed right.'

'It is right.'

It was now six o'clock and the sun hung like a flat orange disc a little above the horizon, and just to the right of the peak of the pyramid, and balancing it on the far side, Abe could just see the moon appearing. 'The right place for a journey's ending,' he said.

'Or indeed to begin one,' said his father, 'so thought the pharaohs.'

Then they were silent as they negotiated gates and checkpoints—one word from Abe's father and they were waved on. Tourists and fans jostled around them, peering into the car at these VIPs. Then they pulled away from the crowd and drew up at the back of the makeshift stadium where there were two coaches, one painted for the occasion with the red, white, and green of Italy and the other with the green and gold of Egypt. The changing rooms.

Jonson immediately got out, stretched and then bent down to peer back into the car at father and son. 'Do you know, I feel much better. You must be the best blinking doctor in the world.'

Blinking, thought Abe.

He put his hand on the door, to open it but his father said, 'Wait.'

'What is it? We're here. Jonson will play and . . . after the game we will see.'

'Yes. Ebrahim, listen. If something happens and we are parted, look for me at the end of the pyramids. There is a point, a line from the great pyramid that touches the other two.'

'You can see this line?'

'No, but *you* will see it. If there is great danger, you run down the line.'

'And then what?'

'You disappear.' His father smiled. 'So they say. But perhaps all will be well. Take me to your friends.'

'I say! You made it. He made it!'

'And Jonno!'

They were delighted. It was like Christmas, Christmas in the desert.

'He's better. The old cod. Nothing wrong with him really, knew that. Got any kit, Jonson?'

'Here, he can wear this.'

'And this.'

A shirt was flung over and a pair of shorts.

'Bit tight,' said Jonson.

'As the bishop said to the actress . . . '

They milled and smiled and grinned and patted Abe and called him skipper and didn't seem to be aware of Abe's father who slipped into the background and who, Abe noticed, once again seemed subtly different: smaller, less noticeable somehow.

Then an official called them for the opening ceremony and they filed out of the coach at the same time as the Italians filed out of theirs and two by two they made their way into the stadium. The Italians moved smoothly, silvery haired, lean and fit, glancing scornfully at the dumpy Englishmen who trotted along beside them.

'Why are you so fat?' asked one of their players, poking Roberts in the tummy.

'And you, you look like a beaky—*come si dice*—how you say—heron,' said another, nudging Griffin, and then sniffing his elbow as if somehow it had been tainted.

Abe jogged along beside them: 'Don't pay them any attention. Concentrate on the game.'

'Skipper,' puffed Griffin, 'you may be the skipper but you know nothing about how to play football.' This, Abe had to acknowledge, was true. 'So just wish us luck.'

'Good luck,' he called, pulling back into the crowd and letting them run on. Jissop gave a thumbs up. The good old thumbs up, and then they were running on to the pitch.

He found his father and they made their way up to the official seats, where Mr Jamil, and the solemn minister of sport, greeted him with a serious nod of the head, and then the sun disappeared, the full moon rose and bathed the Great Pyramid in a beautiful silvery light.

TWENTY-FIVE

There was an extraordinary swirl of reedy pipe music that made Abe think of a thousand diamond-crested snakes rising from a thousand baskets, then a thundering of drums, a great roar from the crowd, and, with one pull of a switch, the stadium lights came on. This is my great scheme, Abe thought, my most ambitious and most magnificent scheme.

The moon and the three pyramids disappeared into the darkness. The Italians in black and gold and Abe's team, in white and green, suddenly appeared in a blaze of light. With all the other thousands of people banked around the pitch, Abe stood and waved and cheered until he was hoarse.

The Italians huddled together for a moment and then took their positions; Griffin and the boys wandered about as if they were in a daze while the Italians pointed and smiled; there were a few jeers and catcalls from the crowd. Abe frowned: what were they up to? Then, even though they all appeared to be higgledy-piggledy, facing different directions, on a signal from Griffin they did three scissor jumps, gave a great war shout, ran to their positions, crouched and stuck their tongues out at the Italians. The crowd loved it and cheered and whistled appreciatively.

And so the game began.

Although the Italians won the toss, Roberts intercepted an opening pass to their wing and slipped the ball to Griffin at centre half, who made a bewildering series of hand signals that made him look a bit like a demented semaphore machine and had the Italians open jawed and the crowd, once again, roaring with delight. He then side-stepped the Italian forward who was marking him, dribbled the ball up the middle of the pitch, stuck his tongue out at their bulky right back, and hooked the ball over to Jonson who nimbly danced it round the Italian who had tried to intercept, flicked it over to long-legged Gannet, who took a gangly swing at it, and the ball scudded across the hard uneven ground and wanged into the net.

Goal number one.

Both Abe and his father were on their feet, waving their arms in the air and roaring their delight as if they had spent their lives going to football matches. Friends at Prackton had talked about going to football with their dads and it had meant nothing to him. Now here he was. He pulled at his father's arm and his father turned. 'Most exciting, isn't it,' he said.

'Yes,' shouted his father. 'They wish to be boys again, do they not?'

'Yes.'

The game continued. This time, at a crucial moment, the team all performed a synchronized forward roll, which completely distracted the Italian winger streaking down the side. The player lost his footing, and the ball, as he tripped and skidded along on his golden belly for almost five yards.

They were so good, so funny. Perhaps they really could make a fortune. And they were going to win. 'Come on,' he murmured. 'Come on. Come on.' He hung on every move they made. Yes, they really could do it, so perhaps he and his father . . .

He looked round to get his father's attention again but something had happened. Instead of smiling and swaying with the crowd, his father stood stiffly, his head tilted slightly to the right, not following the game at all.

'What is it?'

His father frowned at him and then turned and slipped through the crowd like an eel and it was only when he was down in the shadowy space beneath the stand that Abe caught up with him.

Above there was thunder or stamping feet, a muffled roar: another goal.

His father, however, had no ears for the game. He stopped and faced Abe then took his son's chin in his hand, tilted Abe's head gently, and stared long and hard into his eyes. 'Is she coming?' he said.

Abe blinked. 'Who?'

'Is this a trap? Is she coming here?'

'My mother?'

His father nodded. 'Is she coming for me?' He didn't appear distressed or angry, but suspicious certainly.

Abe was stung. 'I was the one who found the photograph,' he said sharply. 'You said I released you from her power. You said she had you trapped.'

'Yes, prison, a real prison, walls of brick, and high windows with iron bars and little light for thirteen years.' He released Abe and seemed to be speaking more to himself than the boy. 'She tricked me and left me to sleep out my life in that cell, but you broke the spell. I know that. I know that. But sometimes good things are done unknowingly and sometimes the reverse is true. Consequences to actions, Ebrahim; that is magic. Everybody sees a consequence. You do this and that happens. A man or woman with knowledge sees further, much further, and that becomes magic. I catch a wisp of your hair, so,' and with a swift movement a tiny silver knife had appeared in the palm of his hand and he had severed a single strand of Abe's black hair, 'and with this hair, I have power, for if I do something to this I can make a bad consequence for you or a good one. You see? Someone like your mother does not judge between bad and good; she does not care.'

He slipped the single hair into the breast pocket of his shirt. 'I think you should go back, Ebrahim, to your game. I have a more serious one to play here.'

The crowd shouted and stamped. Another goal.

Abe's father looked up. 'If she comes she will not find

me unprepared. We have the power here, of the living,' and the crowd drummed their feet as if in approval of what he was saying, 'and so close to us we have the power of the dead, Ebrahim. These great pyramids to which you have brought us all.' And then he drew a long breath in through his nose.

Almost at the same moment Abe's body was racked with a juddering sniff, and no more than five or six feet from where they were both standing in the shadowy space beneath the stadium, the air began to twist and bulge and turn faintly blue. There was the faintest sound of something tearing and then out of this shimmering gap in the darkness stepped Alicia Dunne.

'Hello, Nasfali,' she said. 'Is this your dad? Don't look so surprised; I said I would be here for the game.'

His father had taken a step back; Abe gaped—his hair prickled along the nape of his neck. 'It is you,' he, at length, managed.

'Of course it's me. Who else could it be?'

She had changed, but it was definitely her. Older, the hair no longer spiky and the clothes were no longer that mix of punk and party girl, but smart, dark suited, just the same sort of outfit as Abe's mother and the other sisters had worn. She looked tired too: her face was pale and there were shadows under her eyes. But the rings were there, and the greeting was hers too. He didn't know whether to hug her, take her hands in his, or dance around her making strange whooping noises as the team were inclined to do when they got excited. In the end he took her hands and said: 'You're a bit late.'

'Yes.'

'I thought you were dead.'

'Witches don't die. At least not like that.'

'Is that what you are now?'

'Yes.'

'You are on your own?' The wariness was still there in his father's voice.

She looked at him in her direct, no nonsense way. 'I am, but only for a little while, Shiraz Nasfahl Ma'halli, father of Ebrahim . . . '

How did she know to call him that? Not even he, he realized, knew his father's proper name.

'What do you mean?' said his father.

'I mean that they, my mother, your wife, and many more like them, will come because there is something that I must do, that I promised I would do, and that will bring them right here.'

'Another promise,' said Abe's father.

'Yes.'

'Well, you keep your promise, Alicia Dunne, young woman of power, because I see that you are like me, and I will wait and be ready for them when they come, and there will be a reckoning,' and as he spoke he seemed to change once more before Abe's eyes: taller, his hair streaked with silver, his eyes fathomless pools of darkness.

Abe stepped back. These two people whom he thought he knew or had come to know were just . . . were just different again. 'I saw you fall,' he said to Alicia.

'Yes,' she said matter of factly, without taking her eyes from his father, 'and we fell a long way. We fought for days and for nights and then she, not I, she tired and spun away from me and I knew then what I must do. I have studied, Nasfali. I know more than any of them. Much more.' Was that a challenge to his father? It almost sounded like one. 'Nasfali, go back to the game,' she said suddenly. 'We don't have much time.'

He looked at his father.

'Go,' he said. 'It is right that she and I have one word now. The team are yours to guard.'

Abe shrugged, and then turned on his heel and as the stadium, for the fourth time, rocked to another roar, he ran.

It was half time. The score: 3–1 to the Italians. 'What happened?' said Abe. 'You were doing so well.' The team were clustered together around Jonson who was stretched out on the ground.

'Hello, skipper. Jonson's had a setback,' said Gannet. 'Maybe he ought to sit out the rest of the match.'

'I will not.' And he struggled to his feet. 'See,' he said. 'I can manage.'

'Let him play,' said Abe. 'And win. You must win. Be funny,' he told them. 'Do your tricks. The crowd love you, not the Italians. They love you.'

'Do they?'

They straightened and brightened. Thomas put his arm round Jonson to support him because he was wobbly on his feet, and the others called Jonson a bally hero, though why a hero needed to dance, Abe wasn't so sure. And so, as the whistle blew for the second half, in a comradely group they walked back out to do battle.

Could they win? Abe shut his eyes and concentrated, trying to make them do the moves he had seen them execute before. He heard a roar and presumed it was the Italians. Their fifth goal that would be and now no more than twenty minutes to go. A pause, then another roar. He opened his eyes. The boys were dancing around Jack who was grinning like a sunfish having clearly just that moment scored. Three all. 'Yes!'

'Given a choice,' said a voice in his ear, 'what would they really want?' Without looking he knew that somehow Alicia was beside him, and his father the other side.

'They want to win,' said Abe. Of course this was what they wanted and it was what he wanted too, more than anything. All the years dreaming of Cairo, and the life he would have; all that racing and chasing and the horrors of London; and now here he was with his father, Alicia, and the team and this was the moment of triumph, and it was because of him, because of his great and wondrous scheme.

'But is that what they really want?'

He saw Griffin scan their side of the stadium, seeking him out, and then when he did, that grin and the good old thumbs up, and he was nudging Roberts, who waved to Jonson who, white as a sheet, in that harsh stadium light, lifted his hand and then frantically waved. And then the game rolled on.

He hesitated. 'What they really want?' The noise of the crowd thundered around him and then suddenly he knew exactly what Alicia was asking him. 'What they really want is to go home,' he said simply. 'You know that.'

'Yes,' she said, 'I know, but you had to know it too.' He felt her hand in his and then, on his left, his father took his other hand. 'Watch,' she said, 'and then be ready to do what I say.'

He watched. He watched them play as if they were boys again, as if the years were sloughing off them. He watched them run and pass; he watched them sprint and spin. He watched Jonson trap the ball and dribble at high speed through a gaggle of golden Italians and pass to Roberts who looked thinner and darker and so much younger. Roberts raised his hand and let fly a great kick: the ball soared from the halfway mark, the Italians running and jostling to trap it when it hit the ground, but then there was Stokely, slim as a whippet, streaming past them . . .

Abe held his breath.

A minute to go. Could they do it? Griffin to Roberts. Roberts blocked by a trio of broad Italians heading the ball back to . . . Jonson who hooked the ball high over the Italians' heads. The ball spun, caught in the bright lights it seemed suspended and then it scorched down right into the corner of the net. Goal! 4–3. The whistle blew. The stadium erupted. The team had won.

'It's happening,' said Alicia.

The team ran towards each other, their faces ecstatic. They whooped and then hands gripped together they made a great victory leap, twisting in the air like salmon streaming against the current. Then, quite suddenly, they all began to fade; one moment they were there, then flickering, shadowy . . .

And gone.

The crowd was stunned into silence.

The Italians stumbled to a stop. Looked around. Raised their hands. Called to each other, shrugged elaborately.

'Where are they?' said Abe.

'I found the way back for them,' said Alicia. 'They have gone home.'

'And Jonson, he was dying, Allie.'

'And he will but not till he's lived. All right,' she sighed. 'The game's over now, Nasfali. Look up.'

Abe looked but the bright lights still made a white dome against the night sky.

'What is it?'

'They are coming for me. Look.'

And he saw past the brightness to the moonlit dark, and there, floating down from the sky, in their thousands, fluttering and spinning, falling and tumbling like gloves or bats, were the witches.

'All the witches of Britain,' said Alicia, 'and all for me.'

'Are you very dangerous?'

'I don't know but they want to make me queen bee. Or destroy me. I have found out too much, Nasfali. I know more than they do. They are not that clever really.'

'But with so many,' said his father, 'they are dangerous. I can perhaps slow them but I cannot destroy so many.'

The crowd were puzzled and restless. They felt cheated somehow. They wanted to see the victors, their team, receiving the golden cup. They wanted to cheer. They had no idea of what was about to rain down on them.

'Don't try to fight,' said Alicia. 'This is where we part. Live today; win tomorrow.'

Abe's father smiled at Alicia. 'I too have said that. Will we meet again?'

'We might,' she said.

Then he turned to Abe. 'Ebrahim. We must go. If we run back through the pyramids to the line of which I told you, there is a vanishing point, if we get there before they see us, we are safe. Come.'

'Or,' said Alicia, 'come with me, Nasfali. We have so much to undo. They have Britain in a tight grip. I never realized, and they make everything so awful . . . '

Abe turned from one to the other. 'I don't know.'

His father began to move along the aisle. He lifted his hand in a farewell. 'Yes, Ebrahim, of course you know. Take care. We shall meet in another time.' And then he was gone.

Someone screamed and then everyone was yelling and pointing and the witches rained down into the stadium, twisting and turning, their black cloaks fluttering above them; it was almost as if they were parachuting. And as they landed, Abe saw the faces of some of the men around him begin to change, to swell, become fat-cheeked, sweaty, pig-eyed Lakins. Hundreds and hundreds of Lakins. The crowd seethed and screamed and tried to scramble for the exits. Down on the pitch, the witches gathered into a thick circle.

Alicia's hand tightened in his. 'Don't be frightened, Abe. They won't find us this time.'

A Lakin in the row in front had turned and his dead eyes had fastened on them. 'Boy,' he said thickly. He shoved at the people wedged beside him and started to scramble up to them.

Alicia lifted her free hand and, with her fingers hooked, scratched down at the empty air as if she were a cat. The air tore apart, revealing a thin wedge of darkness, a gap in the light. Abe was suddenly reminded of all the times he had worked his way through a thin gap in the fencing at Prackton in order to set up one or other of his many schemes. 'Are we to go into that?'

'Hurry,' she said already stepping through, pulling Abe along behind her.

'Is it a good scheme?' said Abe.

She glanced back. 'Of course,' she said.

And as this strange doorway in the air flowed together behind them, Abe heard the Lakin howl and the howl was picked up by a thousand more Lakins multiplying in the stadium, till even the Great Pyramid would have rocked to the sound, and above that animal howl was a thinner more piercing scream of rage from the witches as they sensed their young queen-to-be had escaped.

'Mummy's cross,' said Alicia. 'Isn't that just too bad.' And she smiled and gripped Abe's hand tightly.

EPILOGUE

Somewhere near the beginning

1942

Like small smooth waves slipping in to shore on a calm day, perhaps from the wash of a liner passing by beyond the horizon, so eleven boys come walking up eleven paths to eleven front doors.

Overhead the sky is startling blue and wispy clouds drift beneath the world's curtain, slow as dreams. Even in times of war there are moments such as this.

The first boy is Jack Griffin. In one hand he has a small brown suitcase. The other hand is on the bell pull. He has thin wrists, long legs, and a sleepy, secret smile on his face. Somewhere in the house, the bell rings and footsteps hurry to the hall. The door opens and 'Oh my!' a mother cries when she sees the son she had thought was dead. 'Oh my!' and she draws him into the warmth of home and open arms.

And in ten more houses this scene replays for Roberts and Chivers, for Stokely, Bittern, and Thomas, for Pike and Jonson, and for Jissop and Jack and Gannet.

What do they know, these boys?

What do they remember of the future? A frame, a game, a pyramid under a pale moon, a strange girl with pixie-point hair, a strange boy who set them free.